amnesty

amnesty

a novel
by

Louise A. Blum

Boston ◆ Alyson Publications, Inc.

Typeset and printed in the United States of America.

Published by Alyson Publications, Inc.,
40 Plympton Street, Boston, Massachusetts 02118.

First edition: April 1995

5 4 3 2 1

ISBN 1-55583-276-8

Copyediting and book design: Lynne Yamaguchi Fletcher

Library of Congress Cataloging-in-Publication Data
Blum, Louise A., 1960–
    Amnesty : a novel / by Louise A. Blum. — 1st ed.
      p.   cm.
    ISBN 1-55583-276-8
    I. Title.
    PS3552.L838A8 1995
    813'.54—dc20
                                           95-3794
                                             CIP

❧

to my spouse,
Constance R. Sullivan,
for love and for clarity

❧

to Andy and Barb Seubert,
for guidance

❧

to Angela Carter,
for inspiration

❧

and to the Goddess,
for direction

I was walking home one night and I thought: What if my father died today? I was walking home and I was cutting across a parking lot and all of a sudden I thought, What if he's dead? and I thought of how he always looked; I thought of how thin he was the last time I saw him, thin with a beer gut, and short hair standing straight up all over his head, with brown spots on his scalp showing through the gray. I kept walking and as I walked I saw him like he looks in every photograph I've ever seen of him, staring right into the camera with his eyes half-closed and this twist on his lips that makes him look like he's sneering. He looks mean, in his pictures, he looks like he thinks you're shit; he stares straight at you and he smiles this smile that says you're worthless, and you stare back at him and you think: I'm going to show you, wait and see; and you can just see him in there shaking his head and turning his back, just like he always has, and waving his hand like he's batting off flies, shaking his head, maybe pulling his hat down over his brow, if he's going outside, maybe just heading for the basement to get another beer. I was walking home and I was wearing my hiking boots and I was thinking about something, I don't know what, but I was walking fast, and all of a sudden I thought: What if he's dead? and I saw him sitting in his chair in front of the television, watching the game and drinking a beer and saying, *Get out of here,* when I walk into the room, only he always said it in German: *Rous, Kind, Rous mit dir;* and for a long time I thought it was a nickname or something, and I gave it to my bike, *Rousmitter.* And while I was walking I saw his eyes the way they used to look when they were focused on the TV set, watching the game: he never blinked, but his eyes used to fill with water, just from

the force of his stare, and the water would spill out the corners
and down his face and he'd just sit there and stare at the screen
and not hear anything you said to him, and when I got older I
thought maybe he was having seizures or something, but then
I got older still and I thought it was just his way of shutting it
all out, shutting us out and them out and the whole fucking
world out, because none of it had ever done anything for him:
he grew up on his own and he got married on his own and he
raised his children on his own and when I asked my mother
what ever happened to his family back in Germany she only
turned from me and said, *We did the best we could to find them.*
And I walked home slamming my heels into the pavement and
thought: What if he's dead? and I thought of him going downstairs to get his beer, his special pale ale that he never gave to
anybody else, and I thought of him standing down there in the
basement, getting the bottle open, even when those hands got
old and wouldn't work so well, and I thought of his hands
slammed against the edge of the counter after Zach left the
country and his whole body clenched and him just looking out
the window, in the dark; I thought of him yelling on the phone:
You fool, you fool, what are you going to do now? My father
hanging onto the phone, my father, who could never understand that you didn't have to yell, it wasn't like just opening a
window; he never understood the fine art of phone calls. *You're
just going to be some janitor now, you'll never amount to
anything, you're throwing it all away,* and my mother hanging
on his arm and all I saw from the doorway was the water in my
father's eyes and him yelling at me: *You're just like him, you
don't know how good you've got it here, you're just stupid, all of
you, stupid,* and my mother telling me: *It hurts him, to see you
turn against it all.* I kept walking across the parking lot and I
guess the sun had been setting behind me, because when I got
to my street it was all full of blue light, dusk hanging on the
streetlamps, and I saw my father sitting in the dark after he
thought we'd gone to bed: he always had to be the last one to
go upstairs. He'd sit down there and drink another beer and

stare straight ahead to where he'd let the fire burn down, and for a long time I thought he was crazy, I thought he was worse than that, I thought he might be dangerous, and I thought of Colin poring over those college catalogues and my father just shaking his head: *Do what you want, I don't give a damn;* and then when Dan pulled out of the driveway that night with Colin twisting around in the passenger seat to look out the window, my father didn't say a word, just turned and walked through the early-morning darkness back to the house, waving his hand behind him in that way he had, and I thought it was his fault Colin went, and his fault Zach went, and then I figured out he couldn't be blamed for them both, except maybe for the fact that he always liked Zach better, because Zach was big and Zach was strong and Zach didn't take any shit from anybody, and I thought my father would be proud when Zach left, I thought he'd know that Zach was just following his example, telling them all to go to hell and not taking any shit, but my father was on the phone yelling: *You fool, you've screwed it all up now;* and the next morning Colin went down and gave them his name and came home and threw all those college catalogues into the fire, and I thought: Okay, Dad, this is what you wanted, right, this is what they're supposed to do, and all my father said was: *You do what you want, I don't give a damn.* I thought my father must be crazy, I thought he had so much shit locked up inside that someday he was going to blow himself up and take us along with him, but he just went inside himself, he just crawled into his body and curled up inside, and if you looked into his eyes you couldn't see any trace of him in there, he was in some other world, and when I started writing he said: *Do what you want;* and when he saw what I was writing he said: *You're just like him and I've had it with you, I've had it with all of you,* and my mother was pulling on his arm and he was saying: *Get out of here, you think it's so great, you just go over there,* and I was yelling at him that I was doing what's right and he was telling me I'd been brainwashed, and I told him if anybody'd brainwashed me it was him, all those years he raised me, and he just snorted, and turned away with that wave of his hand and said, *I could have, but I didn't,* and I walked out of his house and went away and I thought I heard him say, *Just watch yourself out there.* And I walked up my steps and pulled open the door of my apartment and I thought, What if he's dead, what if he's dead and I don't even know; but that was just one night, and a long time ago, because when the phone finally rang with the call telling me the news, I never even thought about him, I thought: Now I have to go back, now I have no choice; and it was a long time before I got around to thinking about him, and by then I was on my way home, and it was only then that I thought about those pictures that my mother had sent me over the years, of that sneering mouth and those empty, watering eyes and those shoulders set to turn away the instant the shutter snapped.

one

December 1988

The morning air is crisp, daunting, full of the promise of an afternoon snow. I leave my bed and throw up the shades — my version of throwing open the shutters — of the windows that look out over Main Street. The early-December air comes in not only through the open sash but through the windowpanes themselves, un-buffered by plastic or storms. I hate these first few moments of getting up, touching the floor with my feet, groping for my sweatpants, making my way through the tangle of rumpled clothes and cat toys to my bathroom. I live above an antique store, and the owners turn the heat off at night — to conserve, I suppose, though it doesn't show up in my rent. I stand before the mirror and brush my hair, waiting for the water to hit the radiator, waiting for the steam that will allow me to dress, make my breakfast, get to work.

Before I leave, I feed the cat, put the coffee grounds in the trash, turn on the radio to make it sound like someone's home — an old habit, surely unnecessary in this small and placid town.

I lock the door behind me, shutting it in the face of my cat, who runs to beat me to it every morning. Outside, the sun is shining brilliantly, and a trace of new snow lies piled along the edges of the sidewalks — Earl, the man who lives in the apartment next to mine, has been out early, keeping this small stretch of Main Street clear for pedestrians, who nonetheless curse his constant broom, mourn his nightly forays into the county liquor store around the corner, shake their heads over his large, retarded wife and his moppy, dirty dog, and steer around him when they see him coming. The bright, false cheer that fills their hellos fades to grit when they pass by, a grit that settles back to the street and collects in mounds that he catches with his broom and sweeps away, mumbling to himself as the wind tips his battered cap and his little dog shivers loyally, huddled against the side of the building in which we live. All of this I see every day from my windows that overlook this street that cuts its swath through this tiny, Pennsylvania county seat. I turn down the alley to find my car, start the engine, and wait for it to warm up. The sun glares through the windshield; the trees sparkle, edged with a tinge of ice. It does not occur to me that today will be different from any other day.

🖝

My students sit in a silent huddle, impervious to my determined cheer as I stride into their midst and dump my notebooks on the desk and attempt to rally them around me. This is a small state college in a tiny mining town; the administration pays me little attention as I teach my basic freshman writing courses, three or four each semester, one or two in the summer. It is a mindless job and I am lucky to have it. At least, this is what I tell myself. So many people don't have jobs at all. So many of my generation have not found jobs in their fields. The economy took us unawares, and many weren't willing, as I was, to go anywhere for a job, to move their lives to a secluded town nestled in the middle of nowhere, forty miles from the nearest movie theater, in a two-stoplight town with one bar and no bookstore. My colleagues are all twenty years older than I am; they've been here since they were my age, and they've been mummifying ever since. I suspect they think I'm a breath of fresh air. They see me arrive masterfully five days a week, greet my students with cheer, move them to enthusiasm. They do not know what my nights are like. They do not know anything about me, though they think we've said it all.

Today in class we are working on description. We sit in a circle beside the windows, ignoring the snow that is falling harder behind the glass. I always arrange my classes in a circle, putting myself in a desk just like the students'. Often, people entering the room cannot tell which one of us is the teacher. Sometimes I like this: it breaks down barriers between student and professor. Sometimes I hate it. I keep private track of the number of times people tell me: *Oh, but you look just like a student!* My colleagues tell me it's my "young haircut" — young, one explained, because it's a cut a student might wear. Not students here, in this tiny Pennsylvania mining town, but students, say, in New York or Philadelphia. Short. Spiky. I get carded in the bars my students enter freely. And I am some ten years older than they, though I seldom feel it. Sometimes I feel younger, even. Some days I feel that they might have more business being at the front of this classroom than I do. What do I know of life, of truth, of passion? I shut my life off long ago. Who am I to teach them about theirs?

Today I hold up a magazine picture of a woman's face and call for descriptions.

"Pretty," Patrick says, dismissively, sitting to my left in a slouch that shows us he doesn't really care; he has more important things to do than sit here in this classroom and describe a stupid picture.

"Come on," I say, "what's pretty?"

"Independent," Jennifer says. She is chewing her pencil; I fight the urge to tell her to stop. Sometimes my mother rises in me, fights for control of my soul.

I study the picture I am holding. Short hair, dark eyes. Maybe. "Why?" I say. "How do you know she's independent?"

"Her jaw," Heather says. "It's set. She's not taking any shit."

"She left her family," Mike says. "She lives alone, in the city."

"In a small apartment, by herself," Steve says, "with a cat."

"She goes home at night to the cat," Heather says.

"She's a modern romantic," says Liz, a long-lashed woman with deep green eyes and an aquiline nose, a woman of presence in my classroom, as the nontraditional students often are.

They are taking off, rebounding off each other, creating a narrative, a history, which is, of course, what I want them to do, but I have ceased to listen to them. "A modern romantic," I say. "What do you mean?"

"You know," Liz says. "A modern romantic. Like you, Maura."

Like me. Who has left her family. Who lives alone. Who goes home at night to her cat. Who has no lover. Like me. The sun shines in through the snow, glints off my pen. I cannot raise my eyes to look at them. I look instead at the picture. The woman stares back at me, unblinking, trapped in her coffee-cup pose of nonchalance. Maybe I've been using this picture for too long. Maybe I'm turning into her. Maybe it's time for a new picture. The time is up; I tell them to go. Liz hangs around for a few minutes, pretending to sort through her notes. Her dark hair is cut almost as short as mine; it falls around her eyes in bangs. I have seen her looking at me. And I can feel my heart beating in my chest, an insistent, constant rhythm that seems to come from underground, where I have buried my heart alive. It threatens to unearth itself, to throw off its covering of ground and take me over, pump the blood back through my body, bring me back to life against my will. I gather up my papers and leave the room. I will not let Liz's eyes meet mine. I will not let our gazes touch, that snap of life ignite between us. I will not let it happen. There is no room anymore, in this routine that has become my life, for attachments.

The day ends without event; my remaining classes proceed smoothly, without revelation. When I've read over one last paper and jotted down some comments, I pack my things into my briefcase and carry it out to my car. I drive back slowly, take the twelve miles between the campus and my apartment at an even pace. The heat in my car doesn't kick on till I'm halfway home. The mountains click by outside my window, blue in the twilight. I reach my town and turn left at the first light, park on a side street, and walk the rest of the way down Main Street. Darkness is falling already, shuttering the town. The stores are closing down, shutting off their lights. Main Street is lined with pine trees — Christmas trees, brought in and tied into place for the holiday season. They've been there since before Thanksgiving. At first people kept knocking them down; every morning the town officials would have to get a crew out to set them back up before everybody woke up and started coming into town. It's been Christmas here for so long it already feels like February. I can see them from my window — a dozen snow-capped Christmas trees, strung with yellow lights. Wreaths hang from the gas lamps, festive with red bows. I am afraid that when they take these things down the town will seem naked, stripped of its finery. I hope that whoever arranges these festivities is keeping that in mind, that they'll ease us out of it somehow, maybe tree by tree, until we've hardly noticed it, until the town is back to normal, treeless and wreathless and ready to face the long season of no holidays. I hope they're careful, these town fathers, to let us down gently. People deprived too abruptly of their symbols can become violent. I know. I've seen it happen.

I walk along the sidewalk, past the darkened storefronts. Earl is sweeping our block. He always says the same thing when I ask him how he is: "Oh, not too bad." He has a long, sad face, and he always wears a baseball cap. Though he lives in the next apartment, in the same building where I have lived for over a year, I don't think he even knows my name. I don't think I have ever introduced myself. My landlord told me Earl is mildly retarded. "I let him stay there," he told me, nodding modestly. "It's the least I can do for him." I didn't ask him why, just waited for him to hand me my keys, give me my signed copy of the lease. As I see Earl now, I wonder what the landlord's told him about me.

"Hi, Earl," I say to him as I walk past, clutching my briefcase to my side. "How are you?" I say. My fingers are nearly numb with the cold. His gloveless hands must be freezing as he sweeps along the gutter.

"Oh, not too bad," he says, pausing in his sweeping to let me pass. "Not too bad," he says again, standing on the sidewalk with his broom in his hands. He is alone down here; everyone else has gone home by now.

❧

I push open my door with my foot and my cat is waiting, annoyed. He demands his food and my attention before I have even set down my books. I ignore the phone when it rings; it could be a student who has found out from Information that I am the only Jaeger in this town; it could be a poll taker, a telephone surveyor. I seldom answer the phone. There is no one I want to talk to. There's been no one for a long time now. There is a certain power in not answering.

The phone rings for a long time, but by the time I have put down my things and turned on the lights and fed Maurice and poured myself a glass of wine, it has stopped, and I stand in my kitchen beside my window and drink my wine and watch the Christmas lights glow through the dusk. They are still on when I go to bed. They will remain on through the night. I know this because I wake sometimes, alone in my bed except for Maurice beside me, his head next to mine on the pillow, his body fit to mine. He lies there like a lover, pressed against me, his eyes closed, his whiskers twitching slightly. He sleeps better than I do.

❧

Maura — Maura — I hear this voice in my head. For years I have heard it, echoing through my sleep. *Maura — time to get up now.* I hear the voice through my dreams and I shake my head to clear it. *Maura —* the sound of my name is alien, drifting through my sleep like a wail — *Maura;* it inserts itself into my consciousness and hangs there, reverberating. *Maura — it's time.* It comes again and again, through the cracks in my mind, until I get out of bed and walk to my window, watching the moonlight against the snow.

➜

"Maura — I'm sorry to wake you. I couldn't get you earlier." My mother's voice is on the line as clear as if she were next door, as clear and as soft and as cautious as it was when I last heard it, so many years ago. "Maura — are you there?"

I shake my head; I cannot shake the sleep away. It is the wine; I must have fallen asleep on the bed, reading by candle-light, Maurice in my lap. If the phone has been ringing, I have not heard it. I do not even know how the receiver has come to be in my hand; I do not know how my mother's voice has reached me, managed to find me through the years of changing addresses, varied cities. I do not know how she has found me here, in the middle of nowhere, in a snow-covered, gas-lamped, long-forgotten coal town in the mountains far from where she must sit, on the edge of her bed with the phone pressed against her ear, her yellow nightgown clasped around her throat, her hair silver with age and pushed back from her face with impatient fingers. I am so far from her it is as if she were on some distant planet, but I can see her as clearly as if she were in this room; I can see the worn green cover on her bed, the electric blanket pushed back carefully so that she is not sitting on it, as she has warned me never to do, because it might electrocute her in the night and then where would I be? I can see the faded brownish paper on the wall, the yellowed world maps in their frames; I can see her dressing table with its lotions and oils and its dim, white-shaded lamps, and next to it my father's dresser, with its scattered change that I never touched though I often thought he'd never miss it — I left it alone not from honesty but from lack of imagination; I wouldn't have known what to spend it on. I can see the carpet, worn where the door has scraped across it time and again over the years, I can see the full-length mirror on the door that, if the door is closed, must be reflecting my mother as she sits on her bed, toying with the telephone cord.

"Maura," my mother says, "I have something to tell you. I have bad news." She pauses; I wait, feel my heart grow still again. "Your father died this morning," she says. Her voice is like a bird's, faint and warbling, garbled suddenly by static. When it clears I hear her like an echo. "I'm calling you all," she says. "Maura — I can't do this by myself. It's time for you to come back now."

Maura, it's time. I can feel her hands, shaking me awake while I burrow deeper into my bed and try to shake her off. *Maura, get up or you'll miss him.* She is pulling me up to a seated position. *Maura—* My mother's eyes are like mine, soft and brown and fully lashed, like mine, only now they are filled with tears. I have never seen her cry before, and I cannot look away from her, even as she lets me go and turns back toward the door.

When I hang up the phone the room is in darkness, lit only by the moonlight. My books, my papers, my writings and those of my students, lie scattered about the room, looking like cave relics in the half-light. I stand beside the window and watch the twinkling of the trees on the street below; Maurice stretches and blinks on the windowsill beside me. The town is silent, emptied.

She is calling us all. Calling all her children to her. Me and Zach and Colin. We are going home now. We are free to go home. We are given permission. Even in death, he directs our activities.

two

I wake before the alarm. It is quiet in the apartment; even the street is quiet at this hour. Maurice huddles against my side, beneath the blanket. I lie in the darkness hearing only the sound of my heart, thudding within my chest. I must get up. I must get dressed. It is time to get going. I lie still with my eyes closed, making no move to rise. Finally, I roll toward Maurice, cradle him against me. There is a comfort in his smallness. I breathe in his warmth, feel the tickle of his fur against my throat.

I do not know if I can do this. I do not know if I am strong enough. A a long time has passed since I left that small town where I grew up. A long time has passed since I last saw my family — it must be twelve, thirteen years by now. So long since I last stood in that house, moved within its walls, lived there and breathed there and longed to make my break from it. I wonder if it's any different there, now that he is gone.

❧

My father walks into the kitchen when he thinks we're all asleep. He walks into the kitchen and he reaches for the cupboard above the icebox. He moves slowly; his feet with their normally heavy tread seem barely to touch the floor. My mother's bedroom is directly overhead. He has his movements choreographed; he knows every creak along this floor. He knows it like a minefield, knows exactly where it's safe to step.

He reaches up into the cupboard and takes down a bottle of scotch and a glass, then moves to the sink, his feet making no sound. At the sink, he pours himself a shot and, standing before the window, takes a sip. He stands there holding his glass; he does not swallow. He only stands there, his glass in one hand, the other clutching the counter, his eyes straight ahead, holding the liquor in his mouth, savoring its burn.

By noon I have packed my suitcase, boarded Maurice, arranged for my colleagues to teach my classes for a while. Only a week and a half remains before the end of the semester: all they really have to do is cleanup work. The other professors are suitably sympathetic; at the same time, they are curious, suspicious. They thought I had no family: I have stayed here break after break. They express their condolences, pat me on the shoulder; I manage to look suitably subdued. He had a stroke, I tell them; yes, he died right away; yes, it's better that way. And it is. I think I could not have borne it if he had lingered on, drooling or vacant, unable to communicate, at least to the extent to which he ever did communicate. I think I could not have stood to see him bedridden, helpless, dependent. I could not have stood to see him at my mercy.

Get away from me, my father says. He is not looking at me; he is leaning against the counter in the kitchen with the lights off. *Leave me alone,* he says, but not to me; he says it to the air. I stand behind the door; I do not think he even knows that I am there. I cannot see him; I can see only the light of his cigarette as it glows in his hands. *All of you,* he says, *just get away from me.* His voice holds no emotion in the dark. I watch the tiny circle of light in his hands and I see that it is moving. It is trembling, like a flame.

I gather up my papers in my office, organize them into piles, and label them neatly. I am nothing if not discriminating. If there's one thing I can do, it's separate things out, categorize and label, put things with their kind. I'm seldom wrong in my assessment. I am standing at my desk, looking out the window at my brilliant vista of low mountains, when a knock comes at the door.

"Maura?" The door opens a crack and it is Liz, peering at me from the hallway, clutching a stack of books. "I heard about your father," she says, nervously. Her eyes are huge in the caverns of her face, as deep and searching as my own. She takes a breath and steps a little closer, till she's pausing on the threshold. "I'm sorry," she says.

Such ineffectual words those are, used when we can think of nothing else to say, with people whom we hardly know. Liz has been in my class all semester; I have seen her eyes follow me from door to desk, from desk to board, from board to the circle where we sit. A nontraditional student, she is older than the others, nearly my age. I know this from her comments, which are tentative and smart. I know this because I have been listening to her, because I have been watching her too.

"Thanks," I say now. What else is there to say? Don't be sorry? He was a bastard, a real SOB, and I'm glad he's finally kicked the bucket? I can imagine how that would go over. Besides, it isn't really true. Nothing is really that simple. There is always grief; surely I'll feel it soon. There is at least the sense of lacking something, of being off balance, as if I'd lost a large amount of weight.

Liz coughs, redistributes the books in her arms. "Well," she says. "I guess I'll see you next semester, if not before." She pauses, like she's waiting for me to say something, then gathers herself up to go. She turns back to me as she steps toward the door. "Do you want to get a cup of coffee or something?" she says.

It is not the first time she has asked me. It is not the first time that we've had this pause, this moment in which we don't do anything but look at each other, with no divisions or barriers between us. It is just us, two women, suspended for a moment between worlds, and there is such a vulnerability in her face that I think I might cry.

"No," I say. Inside, my heart is cursing me. Coward, it says. Have you no guts left at all? Liz's face falls; there is no ignoring it. She starts to leave. "Liz?" I say, and she looks back at me. "I'm sorry," I tell her.

Liz just looks at me, her eyes level, nonaccusing, as if she were the one with all the power. "I won't be taking classes from you next semester," she says. "I won't be your student anymore." She looks at me, then leaves the room, leaves me alone in my office, alone with my life. My heart is pounding; surely if I glance down I'll be able to see it, pushing out of my chest like a scene from a horror movie. I close my eyes and try to breathe. It's all right, I tell myself. By next semester, she'll have forgotten all about you, and you'll be safe again. Safe in your hiding place. Something about this irritates me. I am thirty years old. How much longer do I have to hide?

I lock the door of my office, turn to descend the stairs. My department chair comes out to say good-bye, watches me leave. I can tell he is wondering about my composure. Or perhaps I only imagine so. Perhaps I'm acting like anyone would act, under similar circumstances. How do I know I'm different? I always suspect that people can see right through me, that everyone is watching me as closely as I watch them. But probably most people don't pay such close attention, probably most people have enough to do just being themselves, living their lives.

I walk out to my car and unlock the door. My suitcase is waiting in the trunk. I have already asked the landlord to bring in my mail, already had Earl assure me that he'll look after the place. I get into my car and put my key in the ignition. The light outside is gray and still. Nothing seems to breathe. I sit there for a moment, my hands still on the wheel. I am ready to go. There is nothing more I have to do, except, perhaps, to change my mind. There is still time to change my mind, to refuse this mission. I could start up the car and turn the wrong way out of

the parking lot. I could head east and just drive awhile, hole up
in a bed-and-breakfast and read and write for a few days, come
back and pretend that all is taken care of. I could make this final
break, cut my family off from me forever, throw them away like
worn-out shoes. I do not have to do this.

I sigh, glance at my reflection in the rearview mirror. There
are lines around my eyes I don't think I've ever seen before. I
am thirty. Colin must be thirty-seven now; Zachary forty-two. I
wonder what they'll think of me. I wonder what I'll think of
them.

🌢

Colin teaches me to tie my shoes. Colin teaches me nursery
rhymes. He reads them to me until I have them memorized; by
the time I go to kindergarten I am bored with them. Colin has
started me on poetry, but the teacher at the school is still on
nursery rhymes. I sit in the corner, on my red nap mat, and fold
my arms. At her insistence, I open my mouth: she wants Mother
Goose; I give her Robert Frost. She tells my mother I am slow;
I cannot do what the class is doing.

Zach — what does Zach teach me? Zachary teaches me how
to spit. I don't remember any more than that.

🌢

I wrench my eyes from my reflection, turn the key in the
ignition, exhale the breath that I have been holding. I am strong
enough to do this. I back the car out of my space and turn right
out of the parking lot, heading west, toward home.

🌢

Hold my hand, Colin says. *Hold my hand and don't let go.* I
follow him through the woods; he moves Indian-style, quick
and light and watchful. His footsteps make no sound. He holds
my hand in his and takes me through the woods; I try to move
as softly as he does but I cannot replicate his step. *Hang on,* he
says, but he is moving faster and my hand in his is slipping and

then I have slid to my knees in the dirt and I have lost his grip and I am sliding halfway down the hill, back toward the place that we have come from. He moves toward me to lift me up but when I raise my eyes to meet his there is only the long stretch of highway in front of me, the mountains hulking on either side, covered with trees and with snow, a chain of mountains that stretches as far as I can see, a dark and shadowed beauty that leaves me empty, because it has so little to do with me.

🐦

The drive is long. I probably should have left earlier; now I'm not sure I can make it in one day. The shadows are lengthening all around me; the air is taking on that twilight hue, that solemnity of evening. The twilight illuminates the snow, turns the mountains blue. I never want to stop; I never want to leave the sanctity of this driver's seat, the control of my fingers on the steering wheel. I want to stay alone with the silence and the growing dark and the night rushing beyond the glass. Somewhere, someone else is traveling. Somewhere, Zach is also coming back, boarding a bus or a train or a plane, and gliding through this night along with me. I can barely remember him; it's over twenty years since I have seen him. Somewhere Zach closes himself into a small space and lets himself be carried, as I am being carried, through the night and back to the place that we left behind. Somewhere his eyes, too, are staring into darkness — not closed — of that I am certain. In all the pictures that I carry of him in my mind, his eyes are open, glaring, ready. He would not be caught, on this of all occasions, with his eyes closed, exposing himself to the glances of passersby. This is the first time back for both of us. It's a first time back that neither of us has chosen.

🐦

Colin waits for me. I think that he will always wait for me. We walk through the woods and when I fall too far behind he stops and waits on the trail ahead. There is never any haste in his face.

There is never any hint of impatience as he stands in the
shadows of the trees with his hands in his pockets and his
shoulders thrown back. My big brother. And as I struggle toward
him through the leaves his hand reaches out for mine, stretches
through the air between us, but when I reach for it, it crumbles
in my grip. I reach out to take his hand and at the pressure of
my fingers it withers in my palm and my fingers close on
nothing. Colin is nowhere to be found.

Zach hasn't planned this trip any more than I have. Where was
he when he got the call; what was he doing when he heard the
news? How reluctantly did he embark? I have no way of
knowing, no way of knowing anything about him. It is all
conjecture. I don't remember how old I was when I last saw
him, but it was too young for real memories. Zach is an image
to me, an image formed half from fantasy and half from reality.
It is an image I have carried with me throughout my life, adding
to it and erasing as more has been revealed to me. It has become
a drawing in my mind, an icon I have painted stroke by stroke,
and I carry it with me like a holy medal. It is all I have of him.
It is the only thing they cannot take from me, those who took
him from me.

There are houses out there in the darkness, along this highway,
camouflaged by trees, by night. They huddle out there,
clumped, still — waiting, silent in the night. Morning will fill
them, coax their hearts into beating again. When day comes,
they will live. Till then, the neighborhoods are graveyards.
When we sleep, we die.

We grew up in a house in the country, the three of us, a few miles
from town, surrounded by woods, in a house with a small front
porch, a metal stair rail, a wreath on the doorway year-round,

flowers in the front hall. I remember walking up the front steps, pushing open the door, the wash of flowers in the hall, the smell of my mother's baking from the kitchen on the left. Passing through the living room, where the fireplace was, to get to the stairs. The upstairs hallway was long and narrow, with bedrooms at either end. I slept in a small room in the far corner, overlooking the driveway, the basketball net on the side of the garage. There was an apple tree outside the window. I wonder if it's still there, if they ever had to cut it down, if it grew too large.

The light outside the car is grainy. No sound intrudes; nothing prevents me from turning off the present, surrendering to what is past.

🍂

The principal stands over me like a watchtower, like a lighthouse, her eyes gleaming at me through little silver-rimmed glasses. She has hair like steel wool and her eyebrows meet above her nose. I won't look at her. I am here all the time, anyway. They send me here every day, for something. I just sit in her office writing stories in my notebook, illustrating the margins with trees and arrows and clouds that look like hydrogen bombs going off. I won't look at her and she shakes her head as she walks off to the phone, but I know, even now, that my days at this school are numbered.

My mother tells me to work harder in school. She is making her bed; her hands are pulling the sheets taut, smooth. *I know you're not stupid,* she says. *They say you never do the work. They say that you just sit there.* And I do; it is true. I sit with my hands folded on top of my desk and watch the minutes tick away on the face of the classroom clock while around me my schoolmates write furiously on both sides of their lined, white paper. *You like to write,* my mother says, *I know you do. You used to get straight A's on your compositions. What's happened to you? Why won't you write in school?* But I do not like to write in school. I do not like that austere space, those faces that watch me from the corners of their eyes. I like to write in the principal's office. It is where they send me, day after day, for some transgression or another. It is easy to write in that office, where I am safe, secure, invisible, away from the whispers. I am safe because when I am sitting in that chair, the worst has already happened.

🙚

Colin takes me walking after school. He comes home soon after I do, gets a glass of milk in the kitchen, leans against the counter the way my father does, the bottle of milk in his hand, drinking till his glass is empty. I wait, impatient for him to finish. He is so much bigger than I am. He is in high school while I am still in the fifth grade, and when I look at him I cannot imagine that I will ever be that old. I cannot imagine what it is to be that old, to be Colin. He finishes his milk and returns the bottle to the icebox, nods at me, and reaches out his hand. I take it and we leave the house, head for the woods, hand in hand. He walks slightly ahead of me, leading me through, threading his way through a maze of trails, his eyes straight ahead, intent on the path.

🙚

There is so much quiet in the night, it fills me. I roll down the window a crack, let in the cold, the fresh night air, try to keep myself awake. I can sit here with my eyes straight ahead and feel the silence expand within me. In this moment, I feel at peace. I am one with the other drivers on the road, sharing a common thing: a path with a destination, a reason to be where we are. Outside, the night blinks; inside, we sit contented in our seats, belted into place, lulled by trust. This road could be carrying us to our deaths; it would not faze us so long as we need not move ourselves, need only sit in our separate cars, occupied with our separate thoughts.

🙚

In my mind, I sort through pictures — shapes and faces, eyes and hair, the moment of a look forever captured by exploding flashbulbs. Colin is always vivid in my memory: dark gold hair, blue eyes, thin cheeks flushed with red.

My image of Zach, though, is like an old black-and-white print. In it he is always leaning up against a lamppost, just inside its circle of light, wearing a hat and an overcoat and lighting a cigarette between his palms. His head is always bowed, his face shadowed by his hat as he draws the first puff of smoke into his lungs. His head lifts slightly as he flicks the match into the snow and slides his hand back into his pocket and leans back on his *film noir* lamppost. But then he always steps away, outside of the frame of my picture, and I can never see his face.

Colin I see in color, yet the details are always blurred: all in color he twists and turns and laughs on the trail before me with the leaves falling around him and the air crisp on his face and then the image rips apart; I see him blown away from me in a fusion of color and sound and pain; the trail explodes before me before I can make it to his side.

These images are with me all the time; they flood my dreams, filter through my consciousness. They never leave me. Year after year after year, they never leave me.

Maura. I hear my mother's voice through the night like a rush of wind. *Maura. Wake up. Maura… Get away from me,* my father says, to no one. *All of you, just get away. Maura,* my mother whispers, and her voice is suffused with the smell of roses. *Maura— it's time to say good-bye. Just get away from me,* my father says. *Just stay away.* Zach throws away his match and steps away from the circle of light. Colin stands on the trail ahead and stretches out his hand. He takes a step to the left and I want to scream; I want to call to him to stop. He steps to the left and the woods explode. I lift my hands to shield my face and feel the heat sear my palms. I raise my eyes and there is silence all around me, a silence broken only by the rush of tires on the pavement, the movement of this car as it carries me along the road.

three

September 1968

It is a crisp fall evening, just before dusk; I sit on a pile of hay on the floor of one of the stalls in the barn with one of the new puppies on my lap. I am ten years old, newly ten. I have just started the fifth grade and school still has that newness, the feel of fresh pencils and stiff new notebooks, waiting to be filled.

The air outside is cold, but the barn is warm, full of old smells, lingering caresses. There used to be a horse, some sheep, old 4-H projects of my brothers'; I even have some memory of a goat. Now there is only Colin's dog, growing older, and a few new puppies every now and then. The puppies are usually given away, but my mother has said that I can keep one this time. The choice is not hard; I pick the runt, the one that ran to me and untied the shoelaces in my sneakers. I loved her immediately, named her Adele, the best name I could think of.

This barn used to be full of animals, but all the stalls are empty now, except for the pieces of machinery my father is beginning to store in them, and an old chest of drawers full of bits of metal and string, all neatly labeled. My father throws nothing away. Everything is sorted, categorized, filed away in its proper place. Embalmed. I doubt he ever looks at it again, once he has put it in its place.

I sit in the corner with my back against the wall and Adele has fallen asleep in my lap, her brown eyes closed, her tiny spotted face exhausted and blissful, her paws curled along my thighs. Her presence fills me, floods me; I sit in my corner with Adele in my lap and the others with their mother in the box across the stall and feel myself wrapped in the tiny breathing noise my puppy makes. From the house at the bottom of the hill, I can hear my mother calling me for dinner, but I cannot move without waking Adele, I cannot move without breaking the mood that is in this barn, and so I sit, motionless, on the floor of the stall, not responding as my mother's voice floats up from the house, calling me in.

This is my favorite time of day, when the sun is just about to set, when the fields are long and time is slow and the day is winding down. My mother's movements in the kitchen seem languid. My father has absented himself with his beer to the back porch, where he goes every night to watch the sun set. School is a full night away, my homework is done, and everybody leaves me alone to do as I want. Colin and I have been for a walk; he has gone up to his room to study. This is my time to spend alone, in the barn, beside the creek, on the fence that surrounds the pasture, filled with weeds now that the horses are gone; my time to spend in some private place, where no one knows I go, where no one can find me, where no one can take this time away.

Being alone fills me with a sense of power. I feel strong inside, my body a board that holds me up straight. Next to being alone, I like best to be with Colin. We walk in the woods together, his dog at his side and Adele stumbling along behind, and he holds my hand and never walks too fast. We talk by the pasture gate, me sitting on the slats, him standing with both elbows resting on the uppermost rail, chewing a piece of grass. His hair is always falling into his eyes, which are always staring out across the pasture. Sometimes I try to look where he is looking, but I cannot seem to see whatever it is he sees.

"Tell me a story," Colin says.

"Okay," I say, full of a pride that swells me up like a raft. "Name three things," I say.

Colin smiles and chews his blade of grass, stares out over the pasture. He never frowns when he thinks, the way my mom and dad do. His face is always smooth, his skin always pink and white and soft, even over the bones in his cheeks. "All right," he says. "Grass," he says. "Trees," he says. He pauses. I can feel myself tense, but I am equal to this. I am like a fighter in the ring, waiting for my opponent to show himself to me. "Hawks," he says, and he is looking upward. I look upward too and there they are, floating on the wind, gliding like fast cars. The way they fly fills me with sureness. I can do this.

"Okay," I say, taking a deep breath. "Once upon a time, there was a family of hawks..."

🐾

My mother calls me until I have to lift Adele from my lap and lay her back down with the other puppies. She doesn't even wake up, just smacks her mouth a little and curls her head in tighter, clinging to her sleep. The air outside the barn is fresh and clear and bright; it stings my cheeks, fills my head as I breathe it in. The sun has nearly set; the boughs of the pine trees that line the driveway settle gently in the evening breeze. Through the kitchen window I can see my mother working at the sink. Her hair is dark and wavy, pulled back from her face with bobby pins. Her cheeks are flushed from the heat. She looks like a picture, framed by the window. I stop for a moment in the driveway. She could be a painting, gazing out through the glass.

🐾

My father asks for the peas before my mother has a chance to set the dish on the table.

"Here, Saul," she says, handing them to him, and he takes them without thanking her, just grunts to himself. I sit across from Colin, kick him gently in the leg. It is just the two of us; Zach has been away at college now for several years. I face the window; through it I can see birds twittering around the feeder that my father fills at night — goldfinches and chickadees and the grosbeaks that somehow remind me of him. I face Colin too; his back to the window, he is silent as he takes the dish of peas from my father. My father always serves himself first, and never waits for the rest of us before he begins. He doesn't lift the food to his mouth; instead, he bends himself down to it, lowering his mouth to the fork, blowing on each bite to cool it. He makes noises when he eats; I cannot stand them.

"There's another letter from Zach," my mother says, pulling it from her apron pocket. "I'll read it to you," she says, and even my father stops eating to listen. I know these letters. Sometimes I bring them in from the mailbox when I get off the bus after school, but usually my father beats me to it. Sometimes he waits for the mailman to come, sits in his place at the table and drums impatiently while he stares through the window, at the end of the driveway, where the mailbox is. Sometimes when I get home from school he is sitting at the table sorting the junk mail, stacking it neatly in separate piles before throwing it in the trash.

"He's doing so well," my mother says, folding the letter back into its envelope. "He says he thinks he'll graduate with honors."

My father grunts, pushes back his plate to show us that he is finished, dinner is over. "He *better* graduate with honors," my father says. He gets up and goes over to the cabinet, taking his pipe and his tobacco out of a drawer. "With all the money this is costing us," he says, coming back to the table. He drops himself into his chair and lights his pipe, sucking the smoke into his mouth. A line runs down each side of his face and around his mouth. They look like they are carved there. Across the table, Colin is gathering himself up for something. I can feel it more than I can see it.

"I thought Zach had a scholarship," Colin says. "It can't be costing you that much."

There is a momentary pause, as if we're all holding our breath. I think that soon the room will lift, begin to float, suspended on our inhalation.

My father looks at Colin. They look a little alike, I think, though Colin's face is without lines. "Christ," my father says, evenly. "What do you know about it? Nobody will give *you* a scholarship," he says. "Not with your grades."

Nobody speaks. My father gets up, pushes his chair back in so that it hits the table. Colin's milk sloshes in his glass. "You're worthless," my father says. I don't know who he's talking to. "All of you," my father says, clarifying his meaning, and leaves the room. I watch his back disappearing in the reflection in the window. "Worthless," he says. The door to the basement slams and I hear his feet taking the stairway one step at a time, as he heads for his beer. The rest of us stay quiet, but we start to breathe again, and I feel the room settle back down around us, heavy with our exhalation.

My mother gets up quickly, pushing back her chair and rising with her plate in her hand. "Come, Maura," she says. "Help me clear the table."

I pick up my dishes and follow her into the kitchen, but I look back over my shoulder at Colin. He sits in his chair without moving, staring at his plate. I see he hasn't eaten.

🌜

I am up in my room drawing when I hear a car horn honking in the driveway. I look out the window by my desk and see that it is Dan, Colin's best friend from high school, home for the weekend from his first semester at college. I watch Colin go outside to greet him; the two of them lean side by side against Dan's VW bug. Colin's dog starts down from the barn, wagging her tail in a delicate greeting. I throw down my Magic Markers and run downstairs, out the front door, and down the front steps. Dan catches me when I reach them, picks me up and sets me on the funny round hood of his car, and he and Colin are laughing, and Colin's eyes are full of light and Dan is tickling me under the arms and I am kicking at his chest and giggling, there on the hood of his car.

"This can't be Maura," Dan says to Colin, ruffling my hair. "This can't be her," he says. "Why I remember her when she was just this high," but he has his hand at knee level, and I know I was never that small, but he is tickling my ribs and I am laughing.

Dan and Colin have been friends forever. Dan's parents live in town; he and Colin have gone to school together since kindergarten. Dan is tall and strong, bigger than Colin, who seems as thin at seventeen as I am at ten; he has thick brown hair and green eyes. It is the eyes I remember, because I have never seen that shade before. No one in my family has eyes like that.

Dan picks me up and throws me across his shoulder, runs with me toward the field, followed by Colin and, further behind, Colin's dog. They often play with me like that, trade me back and forth as they run, as if I were a football, and then set me down and walk with me. They set me down now, between them, and we walk hand in hand. They talk to each other the way they always talk around me, as if they have forgotten I am there. They never guard their words, and they don't need to: I never listen all that hard. There is too much to look at, too many trees, weeds, too many different kinds of nuts lying scattered about the path.

"I don't know," Dan says to Colin. "I mean, school's just not the place to be right now." I walk along between them, watching the night wind ripple the grass in the pasture and startle the trees in the woods.

"What do you mean?" Colin says. The night is so dark, I think it will engulf us, open its mouth and swallow us up, lose us in its blackness. I squeeze their hands tighter, try to draw them closer to me.

"The war, man," Dan says. "We're missing out."

The air has taken on a sudden chill. "Come on," Colin says. "Let's head back."

We turn around, leaving the woods at our backs. Far in the distance, at the top of the field, I can see the lights of the house. It is so far away that I think we'll never reach it.

"I'm gonna do it," Dan says. "I can't take this anymore."

I don't know what Colin says. My mind has wandered off somewhere, followed some bird into the air. I wish now that I had listened to them; I wish I could remember what they said to each other, in those final days of freedom, their final days together.

❧

In school the next day my teacher Mrs. Robbins stops by my desk as she walks up and down the aisle. "Maura," she says, smiling at me. "You're daydreaming again." She stands there for a moment, touches my hair with her hand. "What is it that you think about," she says, "with your big brown eyes?"

I stare down at my desk, silent, but inside my chest my heart is beating like a basketball, a rhythmic thump that I am afraid she will hear. Mrs. Robbins likes me; so far, all the teachers like me. These early years of school are like a dream that must belong to someone else. Mrs. Robbins has dark blonde hair that floats around her head like a cloud, and deep blue eyes that look right into mine and smile. They are like Colin's eyes, but with none of the shadows that Colin's have taken on these days. She often smiles at me, often talks to me after class. The teachers give me a lot of attention. I have not yet begun to fail them. Mrs. Robbins is holding a paper in her hand. "Maura," she says, "this is an excellent composition. I want you to read it to the class."

My heart skips suddenly, painfully. I put my head down to hide the blush that makes my classmates laugh. My chest hurts; my heart is swelling until it threatens to choke me, but, secretly, I am proud. I love to read aloud; it is only getting to the front of the room that is hard, standing there in front of them where they can see how red my cheeks are. Once I have started, I love to read. I love to read the things that I have written. Sometimes the other students ask for me. "Let Maura read to us," they say. "Let Maura tell us a story." When I finish I keep my head down but I bite my lower lip and look up at them anyway. Mrs. Robbins is smiling. "Excellent," she says. "Class?" she says. "Do you think that you can do this well?"

❧

Colin and Dan are playing basketball when I get home from school. I want to show them my composition, I want them to ask to hear it, but they are intent on each other; they watch each other's every move. Dan feints, pivots; Colin blocks him; Dan shoots; the basketball bounces off the rim. They do this over and over and over, before Colin turns and sees me and comes to take my hand.

♠

After dinner I help my mother wash the dishes; she says I am very good at it. "You can see your face in the pots that Maura shines," she says. I keep my head down, my face serious, keep on washing when she says it, but inside I am proud; it is like reading aloud. It is something I can do.

♠

When I think back on these early years they seem to belong to someone else's past, someone else's memories. It doesn't seem possible that that child was me, that loved and golden child with the nut brown eyes. I wonder if I am making it up, if those years were really all that good, or if what came later was just so terrible that it made me forget. I don't know, but I would like to cling to the memory of those first few years, when Colin and I walked hand in hand and he listened when I talked to him, when teachers met my eyes and smiled, when my mother touched my hair with love. Who cares, after all? Who's privy to your memories but you? I can color them any hue I choose.

♠

There is another letter in the box from Zach when I get home from school. I bring it in to my mother when I get off the bus and she prepares to read it the way she reads all of them, sitting in her chair at her end of the dining room table. She makes a cup of tea first, sends me for her reading glasses, clears a space among the newspapers still piled up from the morning, sits and sips her tea, and reads his letters. The afternoon light shining in behind her illuminates her hair. Zach writes on yellow notebook paper; his handwriting is tight and small. Now and then she reads the letters to me right away. "Listen, Maura," she'll say. "Listen to what he says about his English class." Sometimes she saves them for the dinner table. My father reads them right away when he comes in, before he even changes clothes. He reads them standing by the table, his reading glasses heavy-rimmed and incongruous on his slender face, a line across his brow. When he is done, he hands the letters back to my mother with never a word about them, but when he turns to go upstairs I see a look of satisfaction in his eyes, and it stays there through the evening.

In school we are learning to divide; I practice at night, sitting by the fire my father builds in the fireplace. He kneels on one knee before the fire, leans into it, and shifts the wood around with a poker. The room heats up slowly; I sit as close to the fire as I can. When I am done with my homework, I take out my notebook and draw. I make paper dolls out of magazine ads and dollhouse people out of my father's pipe cleaners, arrange them into families. Upstairs, Colin studies in his room. In the kitchen, my mother takes bread from the oven, lays it on racks to cool. When my father is done building the fire, he sits in his chair and reads a magazine, watches the news. We do not talk; the silence in the house is comforting. We all do our separate things, stay out of one another's way. Outside all is darkness; not even the moon is shining.

Colin and I go walking in the woods with his dog and mine; I hold on to his hand, pull at him when he slows down. Colin is wearing a red flannel jacket and hiking boots, and his cheeks are red from the cold. We walk up the trail to the ridge, through the hemlock glen. There is no breeze; even the leaves are silent. The few that are left hang motionless from their branches as if painted there. The others lie brown and dead along the path. There are no birds, no squirrels, nothing but cold, crisp silence. It does not occur to me that things will ever be any different than they are now.

Colin squeezes my hand. "Well," he says, "tell me a story."

There is a stillness to the air in autumn. It hangs like the apples, waiting to fall. It is a crisp and careful stillness which winter will supplant. What is good cannot last. Day gives way to night; seasons release. Caverns open in the fields to swallow the unaware. We watch where we step. We move with caution. Indiscretion will not do, will never do.

❧

One afternoon, things begin to change. I think that I can feel it. I think that I can sense it in the air: that fall is going to turn to winter, that the soft grace of these warm-cool days is going to topple, overthrown by cold and snow and wind. I feel it even though it hasn't happened yet. I can feel the sense of threat behind the warmth of the air around me. It tells me that this season cannot last.

I sit on a rock in my favorite place in the woods, watching water spiders glide along the surface of the creek. Adele lies close beside me, her head on my thigh. I am making people out of twigs that I place on leaves and launch out on the current. I know what will happen to them; I know that around the bend the current will grow stronger, suck them down through narrow passages carved by time through rocks and shale. I know that they will not be able to keep their heads above that swirling, ice-clear stream of water. I know that if they do, they will only be swept by the current to the falls, where they will meet their death in a crash of foam and rock.

It gives me pleasure.

I watch their progress, their descent, with exhilaration. My heart flutters in my chest like a leaf caught in a breeze. I cannot help but watch them drown. I can see from my seat upon this rock the whole progression of all I have created: the trip, the hope, the fear, the final tragedy. Of this small corner of the woods I am the god. I pull the strings. I script the action. I walk away.

I enter the house by way of the kitchen door, slamming it behind me. My mother is standing at the sink, scrubbing potatoes for dinner. She scrubs vigorously; the muscles stand out all along her arm. She doesn't look at me, but I can tell from the tightness of her face that she is angry. Her scrubbing is almost violent. She could be killing the potatoes. My stomach clenches. I wonder what it is that I have done. I look behind me, cautiously, to see if I have tracked mud in from the woods, but the linoleum is clean. I check the knees of my jeans to see if they are dirty, but they don't look too bad. The seat of my pants is probably worse, but she can't see that. I wonder if it's my face, my hair, some thing that I'm unconscious of, some thing that I can't see. My stomach grips and releases; a rush of longing floods my chest. I want to be good. I don't want to make a mistake. My stomach tightens again, but then Colin walks into the room. He ruffles my hair as he passes me, gets a glass from the cupboard above my mother's head, and stoops to kiss her cheek. She pulls away from him, her lips pressed together till they form a single line. She keeps on scrubbing the potatoes.

"What's the matter, Mom?" he says.

I can see her face in the window over the sink. It is white and simultaneously dark, like a day that can't decide between sun and storm. "Leave me alone," she says, and Colin glances at me, full of worry.

"What is it?" he says, and tries to touch her arm, but he has come too close. She wheels to face him, the vegetable brush in her hand like a knife.

"He's left," she says, and the edge in her voice could cut.

"Who?" Colin says. His sandy hair hangs in his eyes. His eyes are cloudy, blue and scared; animal eyes.

"Your brother," my mother says. "He's gone to Canada." Her look at Colin is full of blame, and he steps backward as if to dodge another blow. My mother's shoulders are shaking, but all I can feel is a sudden looseness in my body, a palpable relief.

It's not me she's angry at; my sentence has been commuted, my execution stayed. I can feel the air come back into my lungs. I can go on living. I slip past them to the hallway. As I pass the sink I steal a glance at my mother. Her hands are full of blood.

⁂

Dinner that night is a silent thing. My father sits at the head of the table, spooning soup into his mouth, but he doesn't get it all in; some spills out the corners, dribbles down his chin. His hand is shaking, his eyes are blurry. He cannot seem to see his food. Across the table from me, Colin eats as if in shock, his eyes staring straight ahead, over my left shoulder, so that I want to turn around to see what's on the wall behind me. My mother doesn't even try to eat. She only sits there in her chair, her hands in her lap, the food before her cold on the plate.

"What's happening?" I say, but no one hears me. Perhaps I do not even say it out loud. Perhaps I say it only to myself. The letter from Zach sits beside my father's plate. At least, I figure it's from Zach. The handwriting looks like his, though there's no return address and the stamps are unfamiliar. No one reads it aloud. I wonder what Canada means — all I know is cold and snow and wind. I think that maybe Zach's been sent away to Siberia, like in *Fiddler on the Roof*. There is so much silence in the room, I long to scream, to seize my plate and hurl it Frisbee-style across the room, see it break against the wall, spewing food over everything. I long to see their expressions change. Anything would be better than this silence, this stillness, this closing in of all the walls.

My mother sits without moving, looking straight ahead at nothing. She looks small suddenly, and old, sitting there with her shawl wrapped around her shoulders before a plateful of cold food. Her face shakes a little, suddenly, spasms a little, and for a moment I think that she will cry, but then everything about her face draws tight. She closes her eyes, and as I stare at her face I think I see the muscles moving, just a little, beneath her skin.

four

October 1968

The Sunday-afternoon sun glints and streaks across the square, blessing the bowed silver heads of the elderly ladies struggling to mount the stairs to the church on Water Street. They are aided by their loved ones, who are younger, who push them from behind, and by the pastor, not so much younger, who pulls them in. The church is in the center of town, a small town, the county seat, arranged around a carefully kept square with a gazebo in its center. Across the square looms the county government build- ing, a huge red brick construction with a four-clock tower, each clock facing a different direction and none showing the same time of day. Everybody loves this building, it's a historic landmark, but no one uses it to tell time by.

I walk with my mother — my father never comes with us, and Colin stays at home — and we fall in near the rear of the line. This has become our weekly ritual: every Sunday morning my mother dresses me and takes me with her to church, where I sit beside her on the pew and swing my legs, feeling nonde- script in my pink skirt and black shoes with white socks, clothes I never wear at home. Today my mother stands beside me on the sidewalk outside the church and grips my hand so tightly I think she'll break my fingers. I look up at her in protest, but she is not looking at me; she stands with my hand in hers and stares down a cluster of steel-haired women wearing stockings that still have seams down the backs. They are smiling at her, but something is wrong with their smiles. They have been talking; now they are still. Mrs. Dewberry steps away from them. She is a big woman, with a sharp nose that nearly meets her chin.

"Hello, Marie," she says to my mother. "And how is your family?" There is something about the way she says it that I do not like: her top lip is raised as if she is sneering at us. My mother clutches my hand in hers as if to keep me from running away, but I wouldn't miss this for the world. I squeeze back, to let her know I'm here.

"We're all just fine, thank you," my mother says, tightening her grip and sweeping me through the group of women. "Now, if you'll excuse us—"

"And Zach," Mrs. Dewberry calls after us, "have you heard from him recently?"

A hush falls over the sidewalk; everyone who is headed into church seems to have stopped at once, freezing where they are, as if everyone here is part of the conversation, simply by virtue of being here.

My mother looks at them, all of them, looks at Mrs. Dewberry, and I feel a tremor go through her, I feel it in her hand, welded so tightly to mine, and for a moment I think that she will answer her, I think she is gathering her energy to speak, but she turns without saying anything, drags me behind her into the church without a word, and when I turn to look behind me, I see that they all look satisfied, knowing, and it seems to me that we have lost something, though I don't know what it is.

🙚

News in a small town travels like gas; it escapes into the air and is absorbed by osmosis. It hangs there, invisible, waiting, until it comes into contact with just the right molecules and then it bursts into flame, explodes, and sends a fire flooding through the air. Everyone knows everything, at exactly the same instant.

🙚

I go to school clasping my books to my chest like a shield. It is early; all around me the sky is full of orange and red, rays of color flung across the sky that die like embers in a fireplace, so that by the time I reach the school building the sky is ash and the steps to the front doors as I climb them are absent of color.

⬧

Johnny, from the desk across the room, comes up to me in the hallway. "Hey," he says. "I heard your brother's a coward."

I pause uncertainly, hugging my books. Colin? I have never considered this before.

"Your oldest brother," Johnny says, impatiently. I am clearly being too slow about this. "The one who ran away," Johnny says, leaning closer to me.

Ran away from what? I don't know what he means. Zach went away to school. That was years ago. Everybody knows that.

I am not responding quickly enough for Johnny, so he scraps the politics and brings the confrontation down to a personal level.

"Your whole family's cowards," he says, moving closer to me while around us a little knot of multicolored sweaters gathers. The air is getting thick with anticipation; I can hardly breathe. "Your brothers are cowards," Johnny says. "Your dad's a coward. Your mother's a coward."

My mother — this is too much. I don't care if I don't know what he means. "Hey, Johnny," I say, keeping my voice low so he has to lean far forward to hear it. "Hey, Johnny, you're a dick." There are times when I love having older brothers: my vocabulary is far ahead of my classmates with only younger siblings. Johnny sways for a moment, off balance, then his face darkens, hardens. He steps closer to me, but I shove him, hard; it is the first time that I can remember shoving somebody, and meaning to, and a kind of joy comes over me. In the time that it takes him to recover I have pushed through the crowd of onlookers that has taken over the hall. I glance behind me and he starts after me. I drop my books and turn around; he stops uncertainly, then, to my surprise, steps backward. I think I must look pretty fierce, but, no, a teacher has come up behind me, a look of alarm on her face.

"What's going on here?" she asks, but no one answers. "Get to your classrooms immediately," she says, but her eyes linger on me as I gather my books together, not on Johnny, who is swaggering away, surrounded by friends.

❧

Adele is waiting for me when I get home. I get off the bus and she is there at the end of the driveway, next to the mailbox, a soft, furry ball with big warm eyes that runs to greet me the minute the bus doors open. I wonder how she knows when I'll arrive, how she knows when to position herself. Or maybe she's been there all day, passing the hours with a kind of stalwart patience mixed with faith: if she waits long enough, she'll see me coming down the road. I kneel in the driveway with my arms around her, breathe in her lonely puppy smell. Her brothers and sisters have all been given away. She is all alone in the world, just as I am now. The bus ride home was torturous, not because anyone bothered me, but because of the way everyone left me alone, as if I had some disease. There's that chill in the air again, like the weather's about to turn.

Adele and I walk up the driveway. She waits for me on the front porch while I go inside to change my clothes. My mother doesn't allow animals inside.

Colin isn't home yet. My mother is in the kitchen. She doesn't hear me come in and I don't greet her. I don't want her to ask me how my day was.

I go up to my room and change into my jeans, come back downstairs, and ease my way out the front door as quietly as possible.

"Come on," I whisper to Adele. "Let's go for a walk." She wags her tail at me, communicates her love in the way that she looks at me. She is my best friend. She doesn't care what anyone says. We walk side by side down through the field, sinking

through it to the woods, which open up to take us in. Going
into them is like entering a cave, thick and narrow and damp
with the smell of earth and growing things, rough with bark and
lined with leaves. The woods comfort me; they surround me on
all sides.

❧

Evenings the sky regains its color, then gracefully surrenders to
the night. I stand on the edge of the field and watch the colors
ebb, recede back into the ground. The night wind catches the
grass at the horizon, surges across the field like fire; overtaking
me, it softens, smooths my hair like a hand. Dusk has fallen
now; the day has ended. I turn and leave the field, wipe my
shoes on the doormat, and go back into the house, where Colin
is already in his room, studying. The scent of nightfall lingers
with me for a while, after I have come inside.

❧

"It's time for bed," my mother tells me. "Go upstairs and get
ready." She seems preoccupied; in her voice is a door, half
closed on her words.

"Good night," I say, but she doesn't seem to hear me. No
one seems to hear me, suddenly.

I want to see my father as I pass the kitchen but I can't; he
stands by the window with both hands on the edge of the sink
and he stares at the glass and he's saying something, but there's
nobody else in the room, and it's so dark I can't see him, even
though I'm straining around the edge of the door; I want only
to see his face, but he stands with his back to me, looking out
the window over the sink.

❧

Colin takes me for a walk the next day after school and I ask
him what is happening. He doesn't answer for a while, just
walks along, his face serious, his blond hair falling in his face.
His hair is getting long in back; my father doesn't like it, makes

sneering comments about bums that everyone ignores, but I can see Colin's face tighten when he does it.

We walk along, and all around us the sun shines, the trees glisten, the leaves turn slowly in the wind. We walk in fallen leaves, catching them with our feet and flinging them into the air to fall behind us as we leave. Adele skips along beside us, half running to keep up with us, tripping now and then over mounds of earth. Colin's dog follows, more sedately. The leaves on the ground are brown, fragile, clotted with mud, and some of them stick to our shoes as we walk. Colin doesn't answer me; he is silent for so long that I think he hasn't heard me. I am getting ready to ask him again when he sighs, looks down at me.

"Just ignore it," he tells me. "Don't let them get to you." He takes my hand, tries to smile at me. "Just be a kid," he says.

Just be a kid. This isn't good enough for me. What kind of a kid should I be? Who do I look to for an answer? My father in the kitchen doesn't turn, just stands motionless with both hands tight along the sink. He stands so still he is like a portrait in the darkness. I can stand as still as he can, can hold myself in the doorway, every muscle still, postponing breath until I think that I will drift away, a balloon on a string, and through it all my father never turns, only stands with both hands clenched on the sink, watching through the window for something I can't see.

Johnny catches up to me this time just before school, when we've just gotten off the buses and there are no teachers around. He's with a bunch of his friends, all boys, all bigger than I am. "Hey, Maura," he says. "Heard from your brother the coward lately?"

He swaggers a little, looks around at his friends with a knowing little smile; they shift uneasily, not meeting his eyes. He looks back at me. His eyes are narrow, slitted, watery blue when open, nearly black when they are closed like this. "Hey,

Maura," he says, licking his lips like he's just eaten. "I hear your dad's a drunk." He starts to look around for more approval, but he doesn't have a chance; I deck him with my right hand, clenched, then look at it with reverence. Wow, I think, who taught me that? The other boys are scuffing their feet, backing away, as Johnny pushes himself up on his elbows, a thin line of blood trickling down his chin. I look at him, hard, then turn and walk away, tensed for more combat. But nothing happens; no one says a word, and I walk to my first class with my right hand in my pocket. The knuckles are beginning to bruise a little, but I don't mind at all. All day long I keep taking my hand out to study it. I feel less alone now.

&

I sit in the principal's office, writing stories in my notebook while I wait for her to tend to me. When I hear the door slam, I know that she is coming. I know how long she will take to reach the front counter, how long the women there will take telling her about me, how long she will listen before straightening up and looking across the office to where I sit, how long she will take to cross the room, her heels clicking on the tile floor, her iron-waved hair not moving as she walks, her breath regular, careful, even as her brows draw together at the sight of me.

I keep my head down and keep writing. By this time I can tell where she is in this routine by the sound of her heels; I do not need to see her.

She draws up to me and stops, still moving slightly. She is like a horse drawn up short at the bit, still lifting its forelegs, shaking them out. "Well, Maura," she says. "What is it this time?"

I keep on writing. I want my hand to move and move and never stop, just keep on filling the page, line after line; I want this magic to continue, this magic of feelings, red and orange and aqua feelings, coming out of me like blood from a cut, feelings I have not even known were there; I want her not to stop me until I have them down.

"Maura," she says. "I'm talking to you." Adults always say that to me lately. *Maura, I'm talking to you.* As if they think that will change things. Do they think I don't already know? "Maura," she says. "What are you writing?" She is getting exasperated; I can tell by the sound of her voice, by the way her breath is starting to come in and out in little gasps. "Let me see," she says, and takes the notebook out of my hand before I can stop her.

We both keep silent while she reads. I feel embarrassed, and simultaneously eager. She is the first adult to read one of my stories — will she like it? She looks up from the paper, down at me. "This doesn't make sense," she says.

I take the notebook from her, carefully, turn it back a page. I am careful to stay cautious, keep my movements hesitant, obsequious. It doesn't do to move too quickly, too decisively; they'll get you on disrespect. "It doesn't start there," I tell her gently. "It starts here." I give the notebook back to her, open to the first paragraph. "This is where it starts," I say.

She looks at me, doesn't say anything, just looks, shakes her head. Her hair doesn't move when she moves her head; it looks painted on, though I can't imagine that anyone would choose either that color or that style. When she speaks, her voice is very soft, very slow. "Maura," she says. "You listen to me." Her voice makes me sit up straight, entirely against my will. "Maura, if you don't straighten up, you will fail your grade and have to repeat it again next year." Her eyes hold mine as if she is gripping them with both hands. "You will go back to class and you will do your work and you will not make trouble. Do you understand?" She waits, not breaking her gaze. I know she will not go away until she has exacted a nod, some form of acknowledgment. I give it, reluctantly, dropping my eyes. This seems wrong, somehow. It makes her much bigger suddenly, much heavier, like she's been changed into lead. It lets her straighten up and take her eyes away. But she's still talking. "If I were you, Maura," she says, turning to go into her office, "with *your* family, I wouldn't call any more attention to myself than absolutely necessary — understand?"

She starts to walk away, leaving me in my chair, holding my notebook with slippery hands, but something is happening inside me, something is mounting, boiling up inside, and I can't hold it down any longer. "Hey," I say, and my voice rings out through the office. She turns, looks back at me. "Hey," I say, and thrust my forearm up the way I've seen my father do, an abrupt and violent thrust up with the left hand while the right hand stops it on the inside of the elbow. "Up yours," I say, like him. I say it just like him, and to my surprise, she shrinks a little, dwarfed, suddenly, by all the things around her in her office.

◆

My mother's face as she bends over me is expressionless, its features at rest. She thinks I am asleep. She bends over me to draw my blanket to my chin and for a moment I catch her smell: a smell of powder like the roses that she raises in her garden. It is a smell that is with her in every memory I have of her. I do not know where it came from. I have never smelled it anywhere else.

When I wake the next morning, something feels wrong. The sun is coming in through the window, hitting my face. I roll over and look at my clock. It is nine o'clock. I am late for school.

My mother sits drinking coffee alone at the table. My father has gone to work and Colin to school. "You're not going back there," she says, blowing on her coffee to cool it. "We've arranged for you to go to Sacred Heart. I'll take you there on Monday."

The sunlight lights her head from behind like a halo, highlighting the gray that has only recently begun to thread its way into her hair. Oh, don't, I want to say, don't make me go to Sacred Heart, don't send me to a Catholic school. I have seen the Catholic girls waiting for the bus; they all wear the same skirts, the same knee socks, the same stupid saddle shoes. We have always made fun of them — that is, until I became the center of attention.

"I can't go there," I tell my mother, summoning all my courage. "I'm not Catholic."

"I know you're not," my mother says, sipping her coffee, the line in her forehead showing me that I've annoyed her. She ought to know, after all — she raised me — but for a moment of frantic desperation, I think it might have slipped her mind. "It doesn't matter," she says. "They'll take you anyway. It's the only other school we can afford right now." She looks at me. "The important thing to remember," she says, "is not to kneel, not to take communion, and not to listen to anything they say about God's will."

"I don't have a uniform," I say, clutching at every straw I can think of.

"We'll get you one tomorrow," she says. She looks up at me, briefly, her eyes meeting mine in the shaft of sunlight that filters through the window behind her head. "Don't worry," she tells me, and her voice is soft, lilting, and in that moment I want to run across the room and bury my head in her lap. But I can sense already that those times have changed, and I back away instead, my eyes on hers, until the doorway is between us, and then I turn and run away.

❧

Colin takes me through the woods. Above our heads the leaves turn and twist in a silent, slender dance that is not meant for us. The clouds drift and the winds shift and across our path the dead leaves scatter as if in flight while squirrels fade from the branches like shadows. Colin shakes his head, not seeing the things I see. He is deep in thought, his head down, his hands in his pockets. He might be alone. "Colin," I say, and he only shakes his head, quickens his step until I am nearly left behind. "Colin," I say, but he has gone from me, moved forward unseeing into the growing darkness. "Colin," I say, but the ground has closed around him, taken him in like a load of wash from the line, and the trail before me is empty, touched only by the leaves.

◆》

My father and Colin are talking, if you can call it that. It is more like they are circling each other, like lions, wary of each other's movements. They are sitting at the dining room table, after dinner. Colin lifts his cup of coffee to take a sip, then sets it back down on the table. His wrist is thin, its skin like a sheet of paper; looking at it I think I can see every vein that strings along its underside. It is shaking, just a little, a leaf suspended in the quiet of the dining room as my mother takes the dishes from the table. I watch Colin's wrist and I do not see at once the darkness in my father's face. I see it first as a reflection in Colin's eyes, my father's eyebrows descending; I see it in Colin's lips, moving while the cup clings to his fingers in the air. I do not know what he is saying, I hear only the clap of my father's palm on the table, a clap that makes the veins in Colin's wrist jump as his fingers grip the handle of his cup even tighter. I see the gathering in my father's face, and I think of all the pictures I have seen of the storm clouds that gathered over the prairies out west where he grew up.

"Ignorant — you're just ignorant, that's all." My father sounds like he's speaking a creed, reciting something the preacher would have us chant in church. "You don't know what you're talking about," he says. His mouth is curled in his face like a slug. I see the cigarette jammed into the ashtray before I see Colin's chair shoved back and Colin gone. A wisp of steam flickers from the still-full cup of coffee at his place, a wisp that fades when it meets my father's breath.

◆》

Dinner is once more a silent thing. My mother sits nearest to the kitchen, keeps one eye on the stove, absorbed in her dinner. At the other end of the table my father slurps his soup, all his attention focused on his plate. I say nothing to anyone. I cannot eat — I am waiting for Monday. I am waiting to enter my new school. Colin shrinks in his seat across from me, his back to the windows that face the road. Every time I look at him he seems smaller. Surely he used to take up more of the space across from me, on his side of the table.

The phone rings and my mother answers. "No," she says. "We don't know where he is." I know what they are saying on the other end; I can hear the voices through the receiver, little angry buzzes through the wire, like the mosquitos that clot the creek in summer. "No, he hasn't contacted us," my mother says. She slams down the phone and sits there for a second, looking down at the receiver like she's waiting for it to ring again. I know what they have said, but I do not know who they are or what they are talking about, and I want to ask her who it is who wants to know, but she tells me to go outside and play. I look back at her when I reach the door, but she's staring at the phone.

In church on Sunday the old women huddle together like a football team, with their blue-gray heads so close they bang into each other's ears when they shake them and their backsides stretching out their skirts and their seams crooked down the backs of their calves and their tongues clicking against their teeth like lizards' while the preacher shakes hands in the doorway. And they're quiet as lightning when my mother walks past with me.

That night I hear my mother crying at the dining room table, her elbows on the table, her face pressed into her hands. "She knew I was right there," she says to my father, "she knew it — she was standing there in Burgess's store and she knew I was right there in the next aisle. 'Marie's son, the draft dodger.' Why would she say that when she knew that I could hear? Why would she even bother? Saul?" she asks my father. "Saul, when will we know where he is? Saul?" I look at my father stubbing his cigarette out in the ashtray and I cannot see his eyes.

The sun is setting all around us; we sit at the dining room table as the room fills up with quiet amber light and no one says a word. It is as if there were walls between us, closing each of us off from the other.

five

My mother takes me to the Catholic school first thing Monday morning. My school uniform is unfamiliar against my body; its sharp pleats cut into my thighs, the wool in it burns my skin. My white blouse is buttoned all the way up, my hair pinned back from my face with barrettes. My knee socks are already starting to slide, heading toward the saddle shoes that encase my feet like blocks of wood. I know that I must look like a dork.

The Mother Superior surveys me like a vulture. She stands before me with both hands clasped at her waist and her eyes on mine; I notice that she has no throat and that her nostrils go wide when she inhales.

"I understand she was a problem in her old school?" Sister Agatha says. Beside me my mother flinches; I can feel her skin going tight as if it were mine. Sister Agatha smiles without parting her lips; her words are slow and drip with portent. "Well," she says. "We'll take care of that." I look up at her quickly and think I see in her grim gray eyes a flash of the Inquisition.

My mother leaves me there with Sister Agatha. She leaves me there and she walks toward the door and for a moment I think she will not turn, for a moment I think she will walk through that doorway and never come back. Sister Agatha puts her hand on my shoulder to turn me around, but I wrench from her grip, and in that instant my mother hesitates, one hand on the door, and turns, and we look at each other, before she walks on through and Sister Agatha regains her hold on my shoulder, turning me around.

There are times in life when there is nothing to do but yield. The deck is stacked; you bide your time. You wait, like a swimmer, for the tide.

The hallway opens up before me like the mouth of a dragon; its pink tiled floor lures me inward like a tongue. The doorways pass by, dark holes, the sound of voices drifting to us from within. We could be passing prison cells; I picture children chained to walls, black-suited nuns patrolling with whips. Sister Agatha's hand on my shoulder urges me on, directing me toward the half-open door at the end of the hall. I want to run but I can't; I walk in her grip and it is as if I cannot break away, cannot wrench my shoulder free and turn and run, back toward the light, back through the door my mother has left by. I am powerless to escape; Sister Agatha propels me on, moves me, soundless, through the hall, while around us in its confines a harsh wind gathers, pushing upward from the floor until the sister's habit extends stiffly behind her, outlining her body. Her breasts are huge, incongruous. I can barely move forward against the wind, but Sister Agatha's grip is unrelenting, her pace unfaltering, and ahead of us the classroom door bangs back and forth on its hinges, awaiting our arrival.

"Class," Sister Agatha says, "we have a new student." Her fingers tighten on my shoulder as she pushes me forward. I want to scream for help, but I suspect there is none. "Her name is Maura," Sister Agatha says. "Maura Jaeger."

The students sit quietly, hands folded on their desks, hair combed, faces washed and somber, identically dressed, all their eyes on me. The girls sit on one side, the boys on the other. Another nun at the front of the room is as tall as Sister Agatha. I wonder what they feed them in here.

"This is Sister Martha," Sister Agatha tells me, looking at me, hard. She lets go of my shoulder and grips my chin in fingers like talons, holding it up so that I am looking right into her Inquisition eyes. My jaw aches in her grip. When she speaks, her voice is so low that I can hardly hear her; I know I am the only one who does. Her words are for my ears only; they apply to no one else. "Don't screw up," she says, and then she is gone, sweeping from the room like a raven, leaving me with Sister Martha. The door swings closed behind her, like the door of a saloon in an old western. I picture her out there, unhitching her horse, spreading her skirts for the leap onto its back. I look up at Sister Martha, the fifth-grade teacher. She looks back. Her eyes are colorless, unreadable.

"Why don't you introduce yourself?" she says, and the students settle into their chairs and wait for me. I look at them, in their rigid rows of desks, four across, eight back. Dressed the same as they are, I look like one of them. I open my mouth to speak, but nothing comes; my throat is empty of words, drained dry of them. How can I introduce myself — what do they want to hear?

A hand goes up, a girl with thin blonde pigtails stands up. "Is it true," she says to me, squaring her shoulders like a wrestler, "that you're not Catholic?"

The air is growing colder here, as though the molecules are slowing down, freezing. The others seem underwater. "Yes," I say. My voice sounds like a recording. Distorted. Altered. Not my voice.

The girl leans forward; the space between us seems to close. "Then why," she asks, "are you here?"

They are all waiting now; the room is suspended on my breath. I feel myself choking; I feel as though a hand has come across my mouth.

Sister Martha steps in, puts her hand on my shoulder. It is so reminiscent of Sister Agatha's I nearly jump. "There was no-where else for her to go," she says, simply. Her hand rests there; I look up at her — a friend? Her grip tightens, her fingers turning into claws. "Nowhere else to go," she muses, and her breath on my face is like old wood, rotting. "Was there, Maura?" Her voice is full of solicitude, but her eyes are deadly. "Was there?" she says, and her tone is granite. Not to mess with this one: that is what she is telling me.

❧

At recess time, they let us out into the yard, where we stand around enclosed by a chain-link fence. The nuns stroll back and forth, their hands tucked into the sleeves of their habits. A cold wind blows across the yard. The children huddle in clumps, whispering. The girl with the blonde pigtails, Frances, comes over to me, tailed by her friends.

"So what's the deal?" she says, her eyes on mine like headlights. "Why can't you go anywhere else?" She folds her arms across her chest, steps from foot to foot like a boxer. She leans closer to me. "What did you do?" she whispers.

I look at her; her eyes are blue, wide, blank. A clean slate. Nothing written there, no clues. I'm on unfamiliar territory here; I have a new set of rules to learn. Till then I don't know what to do. I shrug, smooth my skirt down over my thighs, and wish they'd go away.

Her friends are fidgeting, rubbing their hands together to warm them. "You're not a Catholic," Frances says. "We learned about you in social studies." She pauses, looks to her friends for support. "You're a heretic," she says. Her friends stop fidgeting, line up around her like reserve troops. "Why are you here?" she asks me. "Did you kill someone?" Her eyes are wide, taunting. She wants dirt.

I stroke the plaid of my skirt with my fingers, look down at my shiny saddle shoes. Who is this little shit, I think. I can handle her. It's the nuns I'm not so sure about. I glance around me, lean in closer to the rest of them. I look at Frances. "Yeah," I say. My voice is low, confidential. They have to gather close to hear me. I glance around the yard again, then look back at Frances. "She was blonde," I tell her.

❧

"So how was it," my mother asks me as she tucks me into bed that night. "How was school?"

I turn my face away from her, keep my eyes on the wall. Inside me something is breaking. "Okay," I say. "It was okay."

She hesitates a moment, rubs her hand across my back. Something opens up in me then, like a flower when the spring comes, and I want to turn and hug her to me, bury my face in her breasts, feel her hold me, the way she used to, when everything was simpler. But somehow things are different now. We are not the same people we once were, any of us. I cannot tell my mother how it was in school, because I know that it's the only option — there is no alternative — and so I quell the thing that has blossomed inside me, will it to close up again, hold myself still and stiff until she has taken her hand from my back, drawn the blanket back up to my neck, and let herself out of my room, closing the door behind her with a sigh.

❧

The next day is as cold as winter. We are allowed to wear pants under our skirts to school to stay warm as we wait for the bus, but we must take them off before we enter the building. The front doors are closed to us until we do. The yard is full of little girls leaning on each other while they tug jeans off over saddle shoes.

They stay away from me, whisper behind their hands. Frances glances over at me, sticks out her tongue. It's a small tongue. Mine is better. When I stick it out at her, she backs away.

❧

After school I go up to Colin's room, where he is studying. I get home later now; the bus ride takes longer. I get off the bus feeling shaky, carsick from the curves. Adele jumps on me in greeting, follows me to the front door, where I have to close it in her face. I wish that I could bring her in. I wish I didn't have to leave here there, tentatively wagging her tail, her eyes fixed on mine. I wish I could keep her with me inside, the same way I do outside. I stand in front of Colin and feel desperate.

"Come take a walk with me," I ask him. I would plead with him if I had to. He smiles at me and puts down his pen, gets up and reaches for his sweater. We walk down toward the woods with Adele padding along beside us. A dusting of new snow covers the field. In the woods are deer; I hear the underbrush crack beneath their hooves as they run. They are getting fat, unwittingly readying themselves for hunting season. Colin beside me is red-cheeked, his breath forming clouds.

"Do you like your school?" he asks me.

I look straight ahead, feeling sullen. "No," I say. "I hate school," I tell him. "I hate it all."

A squirrel chatters on the branch above our heads and nearly loses its grip, rights itself and looks around, disowning its fumble. Colin takes my hand and we walk on through the woods. Beside us, Adele pants with the effort.

"Don't hate school," Colin says. "It's a good place to be." We keep on walking, our breath taking shape in the air before us. "It's a safe place to be," Colin says, "when you consider the alternative."

I look up at him, but he is staring straight ahead.

At school, the nuns keep watch on us, their rosaries clanking at their waists like warders' keys. I pretend I am a prisoner, my time here a sentence that will run out someday. I keep quiet in my cell. When I am quiet, I am indistinguishable. I could be any of them. I could be Frances if I tried. I can keep this up for a while. Not for long.

At the dinner table my father reaches across me for the salt, which he shakes onto his food like he's trying to hide it from view. We are quiet, all of us. Dinner is to be endured. A kind of station of the cross. My father glances at me, looks away and grunts. "That school costs money," he says, to my mother, pushing peas onto his fork with his knife. "I hope it's worth it."

My mother just sighs and eats her food. Across the table, Colin stares down at his plate. I hate our meals together. I eat as little as possible, take my dish out to the kitchen as soon as I can. No one notices that I do not eat. No one notices anything. We just orbit each other, separate planets, keeping out of one another's path.

"Yes," my mother says, into the phone. "Yes, I understand, and I've told you everything I know." She is standing in the upstairs hallway in her bathrobe, just out of the shower. She holds the robe closed around her throat with one hand while with the other she squeezes the receiver like she's trying to get blood from it. "No," she says again; I wonder if they're deaf in there, those men who inhabit our phone lines. "We've had no news," she says. Her voice is as sharp as the razor that my father holds poised before the mirror. She reserves this voice for them, those people whose calls are now a daily feature. Tinged with gray, my mother's hair curls down around the collar of her robe. "Nothing has changed," she says into the phone, and her voice sags around her words like the hem of her robe about her feet. "Nothing has changed."

In the bathroom, my father resumes shaving. Seeing me, he frowns and kicks the door shut.

Sister Martha stands me in front of the room like a doll, blinking; thirty white faces blink back at me. She has caught me at the wrong end of the yard at recess, a travesty of inestimable proportions. She strolls back and forth across the front of the room, her hands clasped behind her and her head thrown back, one foot before the other. "Maura," she says, and her voice rises on the second syllable and she holds it beneath her tongue like a heart pill, and the air in front of me is flat where my name used to sound. She's right in front of me now, her face opposite mine, her eyes like open scissors. I hear her hands clicking off the beads on her rosary, and for a moment I wonder if she's counting them.

"Maura," she says again. "Obedience, you know, is not just for Catholics." She hesitates. I feel my face flush, the way it always does when my Protestantism is brought to light, as if it were a secret handicap that someone had called attention to, like a wooden leg or a glass eye or a mild retardation. "We agreed to take you because of the circumstances," Sister Martha says, "but—" Her face close up is white and clammy and pinched. Looking at her skin where it disappears beneath her habit, I wonder if the pins are stuck right through it. Behind her, my classmates snicker, politely, behind their hands. There is hair on Sister Martha's chin. I wonder, for one awful moment, if she is really a man. She looks back at me, hard.

"Go sit down," she says, having finished with me for the moment. "Don't expect any special treatment here," she says.

In the yard, the children form a ring around me like lions circling Christians, a ring that dances with their mockery, fueled by their hatred; it dips and glides and shimmers for a moment in the sun, before it tightens to snare my throat.

Frances steps in front of me. "Sister Martha says you're un-American. She says your family's traitors."

I look at Frances with her starched white blouse and her blue socks drawn up to her knees, her pleats as straight as a razor's edge. Her hair is straight too, and long, divided into braids. Her eyes meet mine. We are two warriors on a hilltop, crusader versus heathen, and history's already shown me who loses this fight.

Does she think I'll run? Does she think I'll do penance? I don't know who the others are; I know their faces but not their names. Frances is their leader; probably none of them would be here if it weren't for her. As it is, they're all here, every one of them, all the girls from Sister Martha's fifth-grade class.

"Sister Martha says you couldn't stay in public school," Frances says. There is spit gathering on her lower lip; she licks it away. "She says they wouldn't keep you there. She says that you're a troublemaker."

I look at Frances and for a split second she looks just like Johnny. I look at her mouth. I'm not thinking about doing anything when my fist flies out and connects with it. My hand is back in my pocket before I understand what I have done, and then I take it out and look at it. All around me the girls are silent, even Frances, lying on the ground within their circle, spitting blood into the dirt. They all watch my hand; they do not move, not even to help their leader to her feet. I pocket my fist again and leave them in their silence, but later, when I am alone, I take it out and look at it again. It seems to have taken on a life of its own, and I stretch my fingers out, self-consciously. The bible that we read in class says to turn your cheek, but my hand is faster than my face — I don't have time to turn away.

🖝

The boys don't take part in any of this. They spend their recess immersed in their own games at their own end of the playground. I hang around at the fringes of their territory, watching inconspicuously, enviously, from my spot beneath a tree. None of the girls will play with me; they say I am too rough. The boys don't notice me; they play kickball, softball, dodgeball, chasing one another and panting and sweating and pushing and shoving, and when the game is done they put their arms around one another's shoulders and walk, victorious, back to class, buddies.

One day I catch Davey Janeski watching me kick at the dirt beneath my tree, and for the moment that our eyes meet, his so black and big and fringed with long, curling lashes, I feel a kind of shock go through me. He smiles, so fast I almost miss it, so fast none of his comrades can see it, and looks away before I can respond. He goes back to his game, and I go back to my tree, back to kicking at the dirt around its roots.

My father paces the kitchen in darkness — six strides, forward and back, from counter to door, and door to counter. He stops and wipes a hand across his face like he's brushing hair away from his eyes, but there's no hair there to brush away, and so he resumes his pacing and while he paces he mutters and I stand in the darkness just behind the door and I want to hear what he is saying but I cannot and I cannot see his face.

All around me outside is turning to winter — the leaves are falling; the air is losing its crispness, its subtlety. Now and then it snows a little.

I walk in the woods with Adele every day after school. I walk and listen to the crunch of the snow beneath my feet. I follow the winding path of the creek back through the woods, where I let myself open. I live my life here, among these trees, away from people; I live in every press of my foot into the damp, mossy earth of these trails, in every breath of pine needle air. Within these woods, I live. School means nothing to me anymore.

From my room I can hear the thump of the basketball against the blacktop as Colin and Dan shoot baskets beneath my window. Over and over I hear the slap of the ball against the driveway, its thud against the backboard. I hear their feet move, shuffling right, then left, then leaving the ground. They play no matter what the weather: if it snows they shovel out the court. Sometimes Dan stays for dinner; he sits next to Colin, across from me. His eyes are green and full of life. He eats everything my mother offers him. When he is here there are five of us; the table is full.

❧

Night is quiet; I lie in my bed beside the window with my quilt drawn up to my chin. The moonlight coming through the curtains makes patterns on the ceiling. I imagine my bed a boat, holding me safe, rocking gently on the waves. My clock ticks in the darkness. Now and then I wake and look at its glowing numbers, happy to see that it's still nighttime, that it is not yet time for school.

❧

Sister Martha stands at the front of the classroom, her rosary dangling from her waist like a snake. I wait for it to slither up her skirt and wrap itself around her neck, choke her into silence. I wish all their paraphernalia would turn against them — their rosaries and their holy medals and their scapulars with their impaled, bleeding hearts. I want to see the nuns turn blue, see their cheeks puffing out, hear their voices throttled midsentence: *Oh, certainly not, they don't deserve it, we should never* — and through their words I see my father at his end of our table, I pass him gravy across our plates, I want to tell him the things they've said, but then his eyes have gone away, as if he's pulled a shade across them. The nuns bring the subject up in every class; they never stop talking about it; it comes up when we do division, when we conjugate our verbs in French, when we turn our bibles to First Corinthians in religion class. Their eyes gleam with it. Their voices when they talk about it are a chant, smooth and even: "We should never grant them amnesty," they say. "Anyone who ran away has already made his choice."

❧

I file into Mass with the rest of them; we have Mass at least once a month. I am never exempted from going. The boys wear ties and white shirts and the girls wear lacy veils on their heads. They all clasp their fingers piously around their rosaries, kneel on their padded benches. I sit at the back and do not kneel: my mother has warned me against it. I imagine what will happen if

I do kneel: I will explode, the church will blow up, all the little girls will turn into lepers. I sit at the back of the church during Mass and think about all kinds of things. I go with the lot of them to confession, too, though then again I wait at the back till the others are confessed. I watch my classmates enter the confessional; I count the minutes until they return. Rosemarie was in there a long time; Frances, hardly long enough. Davey Janeski flits in and out like a moth, flicking a long-lashed look in my direction as he feels his way in the dimness back to his pew. I watch each of them as they come out of the confessional, kneel at their places, bury their faces in their hands, doing their penance. I envy them, at these moments. When they are done with their prayers, they are automatically forgiven, cleansed, free to go back out and sin again. I wish I, too, were Catholic, with the privacy of a confessional. I want someone to hear my sins, to hear me, to absolve my guilt. Being a Catholic is so much easier. You're never on your own.

In bed at night I talk to God. He is there inside me as I lie curled up in my quilt in the darkness. I talk to him before I sleep; I feel him in me, listening. At night he is there in that place in my heart where the nun has shaken her rosary, where the preacher has hurled his finger like a dart. I feel him in me at night where I have not felt him in the day.

Colin tells me not to walk down the centers of bridges because they might be rotted underneath. He takes me by the hand and leads me along the very edge of the one we have to cross; it's like walking a tightrope. I cling to his hand and beneath my feet the water rushes between the banks in white suds that make me dizzy if I stare at them too long. I walk on the edge behind Colin with my hand holding his. He is thin and strong and he hasn't cut his hair for a long, long time. My father glances at it now and then, without saying anything. The boards beneath us are slick with wet, but Colin's feet never slip. Beside us the broad expanse of bridge we cannot walk on spans the creek cleanly, deceptive in its smoothness.

🐟

In school at Christmastime we draw names for Kriss Kringles. We are responsible for giving gifts to the person whose name we draw, at least several times before the holiday. Some of the girls go all out for this, leaving each other elaborate hair barrettes, huge candy canes, long letters meticulously printed in anonymous block lettering. The response depends on the popularity of the person drawn. The boys treat all this as a nuisance, moaning and groaning if they've drawn a girl's name, pretending they won't participate. If they like the girl, they leave her candy. If they don't, they leave one of their old ballpoint pens or a pencil, for the sake of leaving something. I watch this with aloofness; I do not intend to participate, for real. More Catholic games; my mother should have included Kriss Kringle days in her list of things to avoid. In reality, I am afraid that no one will leave me anything; whenever this happens there are whispers and, worse, pity. I draw Davey Janeski's name. I am in agony.

🐟

The nuns tell us that the war in Vietnam is God's will. They tell us everything is God's will — plane crashes, automobile accidents, somebody's little sister's death. I have stopped telling my mother about the things they attribute to God; hearing about them only makes her angry. She tells me not to listen to the nuns, but filtering everything they say to determine what is real and what is not becomes a chore. If I think hard about what they say, I can see the problems with it. If the war is God's will, then surely any desertion is also his will; maybe the draft dodgers have no choice, maybe they are only fulfilling God's plan for them, as much as, say, St. Francis was when he became a vegetarian. I work these things out in my head when I am supposed to be paying attention in class. Sometimes I write them down in the margins of my textbooks, the ones we are supposed to return when summer comes. I do not mean to do it, but I seem to have no choice. My right hand is capable of all kinds of things; I have to keep a constant check on it.

◆

"Maura? Maura, what's the answer?" Sister Martha's face is smiling; it looms above me, bobbing, a helium-filled balloon on a string. "Maura, can you tell us?" Her smile widens to include the class. "Perhaps Maura can give us the answer," she says, "since she's been paying such close attention." The other students giggle dutifully. "Maura?" Sister Martha says. "What do you have to say?"

I sit and study her for a moment and I wonder if she really wants to know. I look at her eyes, at the way the blue in them bleeds into the white, the way they're rimmed in pink, the way they blink frequently. I say nothing, which is what they usually prefer.

Sister Martha turns back to the class, walks to the front of the room, one hand on her rosary. She is making a point. This is religion class; it has no limits, no set amount of material we have to cover. It's all free time, for them. "If a bomb were to strike this building now," she says, strutting across the front of the room, "all of you would go to heaven." She stops in her strut and looks us over, fingering her rosary. "Except for Maura," she says. There is no expression on her face or in her voice; she just looks at me, her eyes wide, an open window. "Maura isn't baptized," Sister Martha says, "so she would go to limbo." She continues her strut, back and forth across the front of the classroom. I am seized for a moment with fear of a distant, floating island inhabited only by me and a thousand Catholic infants who have died without the sacrament. I am afraid of an eternity of having to baby-sit.

The nun is still talking; somehow she has managed to work around to another subject. "I talked with a father whose son went to Canada," she says, but I've stopped listening to her; when she gets to that subject, I switch her off automatically. Unheard, her words have no power; they wisp and gather like fog. I concentrate on not hearing as the air around me grows fuzzy; I watch the nun through this growing fog and her knees seem to be lifting higher and higher beneath her skirts, her feet are coming down flat, her elbows start lifting out as she walks, lifting and falling and lifting and falling; her head is dipping forward and snapping back in little jerky movements, and her voice is coming higher and higher and faster and faster: "And this father considers his son dead, and he's a very good father, but as far as he's concerned his son has made his choice and he's dead" — *squawk*. I look down at my desk as the end-of-the-period bell rings and I see that I have drawn her as a chicken in the margin of the Gospel of John.

🐦

I draw at night when I go home. I draw the kids at school, white geese, feathered, swimming on ice. I draw Colin's name with colored pens; I draw it in the sky, a cloud; as grass in the backyard. All I have to do is lay my hand on the paper and the pen begins to move; it fills the white with a wash of gray and aqua. It moves and moves and I watch with fascination as the images take shape before me. Fields, skies, grass, meadows, trees. I draw one tree after another, pine trees, fir trees, oaks and elms, the trees in the woods, trees nobody sees. My right hand moves and I draw Zach. Zach Zach Zach. The sound of my father's ax hitting wood.

🐦

Colin and Dan are playing basketball again. They are wearing jeans and t-shirts despite the December chill and their arms are long, lunging for the ball. Colin's hair hangs down his back; Dan's is as short as Colin's is long. They are laughing; I sit with Adele on the nearly frozen grass beside the backboard and they dance back and forth in front of me till Colin plants his feet and takes aim with Dan chasing toward him from behind. The ball leaves Colin's hands like a bird, drops toward me through the net. Dan can't stop, crashes into Colin, and carries them both to the blacktop. They lie there for a moment, laughing, holding each other while the ball rolls away from them, past me, and all around us the sun hangs silent in the motionless air and touches their hair, touches their faces, touches everything, it seems, except for me, hidden in the shadow of the garage wall.

We are five at the table again, and Colin is passing Dan the potatoes when my father sets his glass of beer down on the table so hard the foam sloshes over the edge, splashes onto the tablecloth, leaves a stain. My mother looks up, startled. "Saul," she says. "What's the matter?"

"'Saul,'" my father says, mimicking her voice. Then in his own again, he growls, "What do you *think's* the matter?"

Colin and I exchange looks. Dad's been watching the evening news; somebody must have burned a flag.

"Why don't you get your goddamned hair cut?" my father says to Colin.

Colin keeps on cutting his meat. He's focusing so hard on it, it could be surgery he's performing. Dan is frozen, holding the potato dish in midair like he's afraid to set it down.

"What are you — deaf?" my father says, raising his voice. "Can't you hear through all that hair?" He slams his fist down on the table.

"Saul, for goodness' sake," my mother says, half rising from her chair.

"Shut up," my father says to her, and she sinks back as if he'd hit her. I feel suddenly small; everyone else at the table seems huge. You shut up, I want to say. I want to stand up; I want to yell. I look at my right hand, but it is small and soft beside my plate. There is no power in it now.

"Dad—" Colin starts to say, but my father is on his feet, kicking back his chair.

"Why couldn't you look like *him,*" my father says, indicating Dan, who sets the dish of potatoes down like it's burned him. "Why are *you* my son?" my father says, and then his back is filling the doorway, blocking the light, and all I can see is Colin's face, looking like something's broken in him.

🐟

In church the minister talks about God and I sit there in pink beside my mother looking at him and I wonder what he would be like if the church were taken over this afternoon and we were locked up in some cell in the basement. I picture him chained to the wall and me having to save him. I wonder if he would save me? I look at him standing up there with his arms on the bible and his jaw looking dark and I doubt it.

Afterward, my mother puts the communion bread away while the other women wash the glasses. Mrs. Dewberry drinks the rest of the grape juice and smiles at me where I stand pulling the collar of my pink dress away from my neck. Mrs. Dewberry is fat and when she leans forward I can see her breasts jutting out where her neck ends beneath her blouse. She twists her head around then like she has a crick in her neck but she's looking backward over her shoulder to where my mother is drying the glasses by the sink. Mrs. Dewberry looks back at me with her eyes round and glowing like a cat's eyes in the dark.

"Do you hear anything from Zach?" she asks. "And Colin — how is he?" Her lips are wet with grape juice. Dribbles of spit line her chin. Her thighs are huge on the chair; they spread out when she sits down and quiver under her skirt like the worms that I chop in half with my shoe on the sidewalk in spring. I don't even think the words will sound; I think they will be stopped somehow by her flesh. "Fuck you, bitch." I say it to her breasts, because they're at the level of my eyes. I say it and I watch her eyes getting big in her head and I don't even mind when my mother catches me on the side of my head with her hand, because my father smiles at me when we go home and she tells him.

Kriss Kringle time is almost over and mine hasn't given me anything. But I don't care; I knew this would happen. I walk to my desk every morning and ignore the shrieks and giggles from the others as they find what's been left there overnight. I just open my desk and take out my supplies for the morning, my pencils and my paper. I have worse things on my mind — I haven't given Davey Janeski anything, either, and tomorrow is the last day before vacation. The nuns arrange our desks in groups instead of the rows they insist on the rest of the year; tomorrow we will bring Christmas cookies and they will play Christmas music and we will all sing together and everyone will give each other the final present, the real present, and all the Kriss Kringles will reveal themselves to one another. I don't know what to do. I don't know what to give him. I don't know what's acceptable.

That night I walk with Colin through the field. Adele walks right behind me, so close her front paws come down on my heels. Colin names three things; I tell him a story. I talk forever, embellish my plot continuously, add characters, invent dialogue, histories; I talk and talk and almost forget I have an audience until he stops me. We are almost back to the house; I can see it from across the field. The lights from the Christmas tree are glowing in the window of the glassed-in porch where my father sits to watch the sun set every night. From here the house looks warm, real; it looks like there is love in it. I miss it, suddenly, as though I had left it forever and we were looking back at it through time.

Colin takes my hand, squeezes it in his own. "Listen," he says, "I may be leaving soon."

I know he will be; I have seen him every night in front of the fireplace, leafing through the college catalogues he has sent for, taking notes in a notebook he keeps for that purpose. But that is not till next fall. There are whole worlds of time in between.

Colin is watching me; his eyes on mine are somber, calm. They are a deep, clear blue, bluer now for the red of his cheeks in the cold. "I want to give you something," he says, and taking my right hand, he puts a rock into it, closes my fingers around it, and holds them closed. I can feel it, angular and smooth in my palm. "Topaz," he says. "To remember." We stand there for a moment, his hands wrapping mine, while all around us a stark white snow covers the grass of the field and above us a million stars glisten in a black night sky. There is no moon. We stand without speaking, and for just that moment there is no sound, no cars passing, no wind, no movement of any kind. We stand hand in hand, while across the field the lights of the house glow staunchly in the night.

give the rock to Davey Janeski in the morning. I leave it on his desk, in an envelope that has my name on it. I leave it there and walk quickly to my own desk, biting my lip. I immediately wish I hadn't done it; I have given away what Colin gave me, and I almost go to take it back, but the bell is ringing and everyone is filing in, and Davey is already standing at his desk.

I sit down quickly, lift my desk lid to get out my things. All around me people are exclaiming, calling names, laughing. The air is full of the sound of tissue paper tearing. I reach into my desk and my fingers stop on something. There is something alien here, something I haven't put in here myself. My heart stops; in that second, I am afraid it will not start again. I reach in and pull from my desk a small wad of tissue paper. Time stops; the room falls away. I remove the paper carefully, leaf by leaf. I fold each piece carefully, after smoothing it out on the top of my desk. I draw this out as long as possible; something in me fears that this paper is all there is, that when all the tissue has been removed, there will be nothing left. I pretend to myself that this will be all right, that this growing stack of translucent white paper will be enough. But when the last piece comes away there is a tiny knife inside, a pocketknife, red with several blades, a tiny pair of scissors, even a kind of corkscrew on one end. I search through the stack of paper but there is no name. One of the girls at the next desk nudges another; they turn to look at me, holding my knife. One of them snickers — "Look," she says, "somebody gave Maura a knife!" The girls all look at me, expectant. They think this is the final humiliation, a girl getting a knife as her Kriss Kringle gift. They want to see my embarrassment, but I am hardly conscious of them. The pocketknife fits into my hand like it belongs there, every blade tucked in place. I touch the knife with my other hand, feel its red, smooth surface. I raise my face, hardly able to see before me; the room is a blur of faces and hair, awash in a tide of white tissue paper. When my sight clears, I am looking directly at Davey Janeski, who is looking directly at me. He holds my rock in his hand and he is smiling, watching me hold my pocketknife. We look at each other, and when the nun claps her hands for the morning prayer I find that I am smiling back.

ꔛ

We can sit wherever we want for the afternoon Christmas party. Because Davey Janeski and I have drawn each other, we sit side by side in the first cluster of desks. We drink milk and eat cookies and smile at each other, ignoring the other girls, who whisper about us behind cupped hands. We ignore the nuns as well, who patrol the room like agents of the KGB they warn us about every day, the evil that could befall our country as well, if we're not careful. I ignore everything except Davey's eyes, with the lashes so long they lie on his cheeks when he looks at me, and the irises so dark they engulf me in their depths. His skin is olive dark and gold with sun; his body like a slender tree.

One of the nuns changes the record; Davey Janeski beats time on his desk. The afternoon is nearly over, and nothing bad has happened. At three o'clock we can all go outside and go home and not come back for two weeks. It is nearly Christmas. Davey drums out a perfect beat on his desk and I join in; we find that by hitting the metal bottoms of our desks, we can triple the volume, make it echo off the contents inside. We are so engrossed in our rhythm that we do not notice when the nun switches off the record player. She claps her hands to get our attention; the sudden silence in the room is deafening. Her face is white, her lips pinched and tight, but all the same I cannot help but think I see a secret look of satisfaction flit through her eyes.

"The Christmas party is over, class," she announces, "because of Maura Jaeger's disobedience." A restive hum goes through the room; the girls are gathering their ammunition. The nun claps her hands again. "And when you return to class after the Christmas vacation," she continues, "you will find your desks back in rows again, because you obviously cannot handle sitting together in groups." She pauses for dramatic effect, and then the bell rings. "Dismissed," she says, crisply. "Have a nice holiday."

I gather my things with my head bowed, my face burning. I am afraid that if I raise my eyes I will begin to cry. Across the aisle, at the next cluster of desks, Chuckie Supulski is pulling on his jacket. I can see him from the corner of my eye. His freckled face is glowing pink; his short blond hair in its Nazi haircut is standing straight out from his head. Chuckie Supulski stutters. He is slightly overweight. Before I came along, he used to be the butt of class jokes — Chuckie Supulski smells; Chuckie Supulski is an only child — this being, in Catholic logic, a serious transgression. Now he stands across the aisle from me tugging his jacket up over his mittens and his nose is running.

"Shit," he says, daringly, first glancing over his shoulder to be sure that none of the nuns is near him. "Maura'll probably ruin our whole Christmas." I cannot stop myself; the tears are welling over in my eyes. Blindly, I reach for my jacket. The others around us nod in agreement and he says it again, louder. "Maura ruins everything. And she's not even Catholic." The others nod approvingly.

Encouraged, Chuckie steps nearer to me. "Hey, Maura," he whispers, "seen your brother lately?" I raise my head; instinctively my right hand tightens on the pocketknife. I turn to face him, but Davey Janeski has thrust himself between us.

"Shut up," he says to Chuckie Supulski, loudly, clearly. "Leave her alone. She's not going to ruin anything." Chuckie steps back, astonished, and the others follow suit. No one has ever taken my part before. Davey Janeski takes my hand and leads me from the classroom, walks me to my bus. "Merry

Christmas," he says, not looking at me, and before I can recover, he is gone.

❧

I want to show Colin the pocketknife, but I'm afraid he will ask about the stone. We are making our way with the dogs down through the snow on the path beyond the creek when he stops suddenly, touches a tree with his fingers. He shakes his head. I stand waiting, while around us the air grows colder, as if reacting to our lack of movement. He shows me where the bark of the tree has been cut to form someone's initials. "Never do that," he tells me. "It kills the tree." We stand for a moment, as if in prayer. I finger the knife in my right-hand pocket and feel guilty by association.

❧

In church the preacher reads aloud the names of the congregation's sons who have enlisted while my mother sits ramrod-straight in the pew beside me. When we stand for the recessional hymn, I sense something is different. I look quickly at my mother from under the cover of my hymnal. She is not singing, just moving her mouth to the words.

In Sunday school Mary whispers to me that my brother's a coward. I tackle her afterwards; she has blonde pigtails that I grab and twist from her head till her eyes bulge out even more than they already do. Little tears spill from both her eyes and I smack them on her cheeks like flies until my mother has my collar in one hand and my ear in the other, shaking me till I think I won't be able to hear anymore, but still with one foot I'm kicking at this girl with her face in her mother's skirt.

❧

Dan comes over that same afternoon. I answer the door when he knocks and his face is stiff and careful. "Hey, Maurie," he says, but he doesn't really seem to see me. He is looking past me through the open door. Colin comes up behind me.

"Hey, man," Dan says, but there's none of his usual bravado in it.

"Hey," Colin says, reaching into the closet for his jacket. He slips past me and goes outside. I get my jacket and go outside, too. I'm not missing anything.

We all walk along without speaking for a while, the dogs at our heels. The cold air stings our cheeks, the snow crunches beneath our feet.

"What's up?" Colin says.

Dan takes a breath, exhales, and looks up at the sky. A hawk glides overhead, buzzardlike. It could be circling us, stalking its prey. "I'm dropping out of college," Dan says, not looking at us. "I joined up," he says. We all stop, simultaneously. "I joined the Marines," Dan says. "I can't take it anymore." He and Colin look at each other. Overhead the hawk glides, dropping on the air. "I can't take being here," Dan says. His eyes are as green as lake water. There are freckles on his cheeks. I don't think I ever noticed them before.

Colin looks away from him, puts his hands in his pockets, stares into the woods.

"It's nothing to do with you, man," Dan says. "Go to college," he says, but Colin keeps on staring at the trees, like he's expecting something to come out of them and when it does he's going to be ready for it. "You gotta do what's right for you," Dan says, but I don't know if Colin's even listening to him anymore.

My father sits in his chair on the back porch and stares straight ahead into the sunset, one hand on his glass of beer, the other gripping the arm of his chair. He stares straight ahead and the blue of his eyes is faded almost white. He sits and he blinks to clear the water from his eyes and my mother in the other room is crisp on the phone. "No," she says, "we don't know where he is. No, we have no forwarding address. No," and her voice tightens into steel, "I told you the last time you called. We have no idea where he is." It is like a litany; I almost have it memorized. I sit by the fire and I play with my paper dolls and beside me Colin sorts through his college catalogues, pretending not to hear.

&

More and more these days I go into the woods without Colin. He is always busy, always has homework. He is too busy even to play basketball, and sometimes Dan comes over and plays alone; I hear him dribbling the ball while I change my clothes after school. I go into the woods alone, except for Adele, watch the shadows turn to evening. Adele sits beside me, snuggles against my side. I put my arm around her. I can feel her breathing, her sides moving in and out against me. She licks her chops a few times, pushes her head against my chest. We sit like that for a while, Adele's warm body tight against mine, the leaves around us lying dead on the ground, and I think of Colin, wish that he were here.

&

"How many brothers do *you* have, Maura?" We are telling about our families in social studies, as if we don't already know everything about each other, and everybody else in this town. "How many children in *your* family?" Sister Martha is bending down toward me, her face a mask of concern.

There is one picture of the three of us, hanging on the wall above my mother's dresser. Colin and Zachary are kneeling behind Colin's dog. Colin's face is all angles, his skin so white it looks like bone. His eyes are big and blue and soft under a baseball cap pulled down over his brow. He is looking off into the distance, one hand on the dog's collar, the other beneath its jaw, his fingers clotted with its saliva. Behind Colin, Zachary glares right into the camera; his straight black hair sticks out from his head and his teeth protrude a little in front. His hands are balled up into fists and he looks ready to leap right out of the frame. His eyes in the light of my mother's room look brown. I am sitting on the ground beside Colin and Zach, a little apart. I must be two or three; my face is in the shade and it is impossible to tell anything about me.

"How many brothers, Maura?" Sister Martha asks, lisping slightly. I hate her teeth, yellowed teeth that never see the light; her tongue clicking against them makes them sound like they're all loose in their gums. I think if this were medieval times her teeth would fall out soon. "How many brothers, Maura?" She is losing patience. If I am silent long enough she'll have to move on. If this were medieval times, I could cast a spell on them, and Zachary would come home on a horse, carrying a shield and wearing armor.

The days are so short now we seem to move in eternal darkness. By the time I get home from school the shadows are long across the field and the moon is out and glowing in one corner of the sky. I come home from school and Adele meets me at the end of the driveway and we walk in the woods immediately, taking long steps as if to beat the darkness that is settling subtly all around me like sifted flour. When I get back home my mother is in the kitchen and dinner is nearly ready. I leave Adele on the front porch, in the cold. We eat in silence nearly all the time now, and when the meal is over I clear the dishes from the table and help my mother stack them in the dishwasher. Colin goes to his room to study, and I go to mine. There is so little conversation between us it is like living in a morgue. I think we are entombed within these walls, in a grave of our own making.

When my father swallows he tilts his head back, looks away from the window, and closes his eyes, for just the time it takes to swallow; then his head drops down again. He is still for a moment and then he lifts his glass again and swallows the rest, sets the glass down, and stands with both hands gripping the counter, his head tipped back, his eyes closed in the darkness, shutting us out.

When my father and Colin do talk, it is only as prelude to a fight. Everything about Colin is wrong — the way he stands, slouching with his back bent; the length of his hair; the ragged beard he is trying to grow. He doesn't keep his room clean, he doesn't keep himself clean, doesn't clean his fingernails. He doesn't take care of himself, and that, in my father's eyes, seems to be the greatest sin. When my father was Colin's age, he was starting a family. Colin has turned eighteen, but seems barely capable of supporting himself in my father's eyes. Whenever Colin tries to talk, my father waves him away. When Colin asks him for advice with the college catalogues, my father shakes his head. "Do what you want," he says, low, sitting motionless in his chair. "Do whatever the hell you want," he says. "I don't give a damn."

🍂

I used to think sometimes that I could go back home and stand in the kitchen late at night and my father would offer me a shot of whiskey, and we'd stand there with our hips against the counter, side by side, and talk. I used to think that I could do that. I thought that he might listen to me, late at night, on his turf, thought we might exchange confidences. I used to think that he might tell me, if I listened to him, why he did what he did.

🍂

The phone rings late at night, so late that we are all in bed. I lie beneath my quilt and listen to my mother in the hallway picking up the receiver. There is a quaver in her voice when she says hello, as if she is expecting bad news. There is a long silence, a long absence of sound, after she says hello, and when I creep to the doorway and look out I see her standing there with one hand pressed against her mouth, bunched into a fist. I see she is trying to collect herself, to gain control. "Oh, Zach," she whispers, finally, into the receiver, "where are you?"

My father shoulders into the hallway; he doesn't even seem to see me, just pushes past and takes the receiver out of my mother's hand. For a moment I am afraid that he will hang it up, cut off the connection, but instead he lifts it to his ear and starts to yell. "You fool, you fool," he says, "what are you going to do now? You've thrown it all away!" My father's voice is shaking, like he's had a lot to drink; his face is shaking, tears are rolling down, and he is yelling at the receiver in his hand as if it were to blame. "You'll never amount to anything now," he yells, "you're just going to be some janitor now." My father's face is shaking, his voice is shaking, dropping to a whisper I can barely hear. "You've screwed it all up now," my father whispers, "you've got no home here anymore. You fool," he says, so softly it might be my mother's voice. "You goddamned fool."

My mother doesn't move when my father hangs up the phone. She stays slumped in the chair in the hallway, her hand bunched up against her mouth, not saying a word while my father treads his heavy tread into the kitchen and reaches up into his cupboard. There is silence for a moment, and then I smell the fire, now, in the middle of the night, and I run down into the living room, and Colin is on his knees in front of the fireplace, burning all those college catalogues, just as if they were wood.

For weeks, I live with Adele. She waits for me at the end of the driveway after school and we go for walks together. She sits with me beside the creek, her brown eyes liquid and fixed on mine. She listens to every word I say. I put my arms around her neck and bury my face in her fur, breathe in her smell. She is warm and familiar, a solid presence in my arms. We wait, together, for Colin.

When Colin comes back from boot camp, it is my mother who opens the door, and when she comes into the living room I think her face is made of glass that will shatter if I speak. Colin comes in behind her and for a moment I don't recognize him;

he's wearing a uniform and his hair is cut so short he looks like someone else. He doesn't look at me, just sits down beside my father in the living room. They sit there not talking, my father all straight and stiff in his chair, with his hand around a glass of beer, and Colin's gaze darting all over the room, his eyes flitting back and forth in his head like gnats. I look at his hands on the arms of his chair, and his knuckles are leaping out of them as white as his face. I sit with my head down and my eyes focused on Colin's boots thinking that the uniform's got him shut up like a box, not letting him talk.

"Get up," my mother says. "Get up; it's time." Her face as she bends over me is closed and grim. "Maura," she says, "they're leaving now," and I lie still while her hands tug at my shoulders; I lie absolutely still with the quilt pulled up to my chin, feigning sleep.

Dan comes and gets Colin in his car that glides up the driveway like a sled, like the toboggans we used to take down the pasture after dark in the winter, Colin holding me with his knees. From the window in the kitchen, I watch Dan pulling in and I think of pouring pails of water down the driveway in winter with Colin so that it would freeze and make my sled move faster. I think of my father's shoulders when we did that. They rose up around his neck as his head settled in and his eyebrows knotted together and my mother said, "Your father doesn't like it when you do that, dear." I watch Dan get out of his car; his uniform matches Colin's.

Colin and Dan drive away as I wave from the porch. They drive down the driveway with Colin twisting around in the seat next to Dan to wave back. I see his face for just a second through the back window before they pull away. Dan taps on the horn and it calls to me as I watch them disappear between the trees. I stand there for a moment and the driveway looms up empty while behind me my parents walk back into the house.

The sound of the horn bends, stretches toward me across the fields. It hangs in midair, one note suspended through time, hovering for a long moment before it swoops and leaves me and disappears into the distance and I am left with the silence of a windless field.

seven ───────────────────────────────────────

March 1970

It is two years later, nearly spring. The winter months are winding down. I can feel the warmth pushing through the cold, like the flowers pushing through the ground. I can feel it coming everywhere. The water rushes through the creek, forming little rapids within its banks. I sit on my rock beside the creek and watch it flow, watch the little buds beginning to ease out along the branches of the trees, feel the sunlight become warm again. Adele sits beside me, her head against my shoulder, breathing in my ear. Her breath smells bad, but I don't care. I wrap my arms around her and hold her close to me, kiss the top of her head. She pants against me. "Hey, Adele," I whisper. "Name three things." But she only looks at me, wags her tail against the rock. She is only a dog. She is just company.

She watches me play with my pipe cleaners, sits there on the rock with me while I twist them into human shapes, give them bits of curled ribbon for hair, clothe them in fabric scraps discarded from my mother's sewing. Dozens of tiny people are scattered on the rock around me. I give them names and histories; I write scripts for them. I group them into families, assign them roles. I sit on this rock throughout the spring and the wind lifts my hair and touches my cheek and the trees around me rise like soldiers from the dirt. I sit my pipe cleaner people on leaf boats and send them down the creek, watching them pass between the water spiders that knife across the surface like ice skaters, watching them drift downstream, toward the waterfall.

"Sweden has the highest suicide rate in the world," Sister Rosaria tells us in seventh-grade social studies, aiming her pointer at the map. She could be holding a gun. "And do you know why?" She waits, tapping her pointer against the toe of her shoe. Slouched down in my seat with my arms folded across my chest, I couldn't care less. Sister Rosaria nods, satisfied with our innocent ignorance. We are so lucky, not to know. "It's because they have socialism," she says. Her smile splits her face like a wound. "They pay fifty percent of their salaries in taxes." I watch the rest of them around me taking notes and I wait for the bell to sound. I've had it with this shit. As far as I'm concerned, I'm just biding my time. As soon as summer comes, I'm out of here, busting over that fence and taking off, flying over their heads into the sky, soaring like a hawk.

I'm so busy being nonchalant that I don't even see the hand go up. Sister Rosaria doesn't see it at first either; she's so unused to participation. But the hand is waving, determinedly. "Excuse me," a voice says.

Sister Rosaria recovers herself. "Yes?" she says, trying to look receptive. Her smile's got a waver in it, like static on a TV screen.

A girl stands up, a tall girl with thick dark hair that hangs down her back, wisps of it escaping her barrettes around her hairline. Have I seen her before?

"She's new," Frances whispers from across the aisle. "She just transferred here."

The new girl stands there with her arms folded, her head to one side. The pleats in her skirt don't hang quite straight in the back; she's got an ass. Her pullover is tight across her chest, showing two round mounds beneath the wool. The boys nudge one another on their side of the classroom. "Isn't their suicide rate high because of light deprivation?" she says.

I sit up straighter. Who is this girl? Where did she come from? She stands there with her head thrown back and her eyes on Sister Rosaria like she's challenging her to a duel.

Sister Rosaria coughs a little, behind her hand. "Sit down, Magdelene," she says. "We're moving on to Russia now."

Magdelene sits down, her skirt flouncing around her, cups her chin in her hand. She yawns, bored, and looks around the room. Her eyes meet mine. Her eyes are green; I can tell even from here. They are large and green and full of scorn. I stare at her, mesmerized. Magdelene. I can feel my life change, in that moment, as if by sacrament. It's like I've been born again, received my first communion, been bat mitzvahed, all in one clear moment. It's an ecumenical experience. Magdelene looks at me, a long and silky look. Her skin is smooth and olive-toned. Her mouth looks like a rosebud. She winks at me.

It's like flying, without even leaving my chair.

❦

At recess, Magdelene comes over to me. "You want a cigarette?" she says.

"Sure," I say. I try to look like I smoke all the time, following her to the edge of the yard, out of sight of the nuns.

Things have changed around here these past two years. Everyone is nicer to us now. People tip their hats to us in church. Frances stays away from me at recess. The town glows all around us, rolling hills and woods and church spires nestled into neighborhoods. Everything sparkles, freshly varnished. Everyone seems happy now, but my mother still doesn't sing the hymns in church, and I stand beside her, moving my lips in support.

Colin's being in Vietnam has given me a new status in school. I am the only one who has a brother who is actually in Vietnam, and the others give me space on the playground. Nobody mentions Zach anymore. Once in a while I catch the sisters looking at me in a way they never have before. It is a look that takes me in, a look almost of pity. I suspect it is the closest they come to sympathy, but it is a look I cannot bear — being ostracized was almost better. Now I almost feel like we are on the same side, and such an allegiance somehow terrifies me.

Magdelene slips the cigarette between her lips, lights it, and draws the smoke into her lungs with a fierceness that is daunting. She hands it to me. I put it to my mouth and inhale. I feel like I've swallowed lye. I'm doubled up, choking and coughing, before I know it. Magdelene just watches me, leaning up against the wall. I glance at her as I catch my breath, feeling ashamed. She looks amused. "Don't worry," she says. "You'll catch on."

She finishes the cigarette on her own. I lean up against the wall beside her and just watch her. The sharp spring air blows her hair back from her eyes, exposing her skin to the sun.

We hear from Colin now and then. Sometimes he calls; now and then he writes. I see pictures of Vietnam in the news every day, on TV every night. I hear about it all the time. I no longer sleep at night; when I try, Colin is there. All night he screams in my head, and when I curl into my bed and press into the space my body has made and hold my blanket to my chin with my fists, all I can feel is his scream around me, filling my room till there's no more space to breathe. I try to feel the way I used to feel at night before sleep. I lie in bed and try to talk to God, but I am empty inside. There is nothing in me anymore. Nothing is in me, listening.

For a while I think I am waiting for them, for Zach and Colin to come home. For some reason, I think of them now as being in the same place, though I know that Colin is in Vietnam and Zach is not. There is no one here to tell my stories to. There is no one left to listen. Adele lies beside me with her head on her paws, her eyes closed. She can't understand me. Not really. And Colin's dog never leaves the barn anymore, just stays in there in the corner of one of the stalls, nesting in the hay. I never see her eat. I sit on my rock beside the creek and play with the leaves and sticks and bits of bark and all around me I hear sounds inside the shadows, and I think that if I can lift my head fast enough I'll see them, Zach and Colin, darting out of sight behind a tree, and I'll know at least which way to go to try to find them.

♪

The nuns tell us stories about the saints. They tell them during quiet time, as we sit with our hands folded on top of our desks — always visible; I don't know what they think we might do, out of sight beneath our desks — fumble beneath our skirts? Rouse ourselves to tales of flagellation?

"The three children of Fatima were blessed," Sister Rosaria tells us. This is her favorite story. The oldest child, Lucy, used to tie a knotted rope around her waist, beneath her clothes, as penance. When the others found it, stained with blood beside her unconscious body, they fought over who would get to wear it next.

Saint Therese found spiritual orgasm in consumption; her colleagues drank her spittle. Saint Joan gave herself up to burning at the stake. The sisters love these stories; they tell them again and again. I think about them, on my own, late at night: these women with their private and public penances. Something always comes of it for them — after life, at least, if not during. God listens to them, at any rate; somehow they've gotten to him. At night, after my parents have gone to bed, I stand before the mirror in the bathroom with the door locked and try it out myself, repeatedly slam my fist into my face. It is an awkward movement, but it is the only method I can think of. I stand before the mirror, impatient because my skin refuses to bruise. I never dare to strike too hard, for fear of waking my parents. Not being Catholic, they would not understand. I want the bruises. I want to wear them like medals, like Lucy's knotted rope. A proof of something. I stand before the mirror and systematically strike my face and think: I am doing this for God. Maybe he'll take note, come back into my life again. For what purpose, I do not know. For Zach, for Colin — the reason isn't

clear. As a kind of absolution. A secular penance. The sins of
the brothers shall be visited on their sisters. I do not know my
rationale, I only stand and watch my cheeks turn red, my eyes
round and open and empty of expression in the mirror, blinking
only when my fist makes contact with my flesh, as I wait
impatiently for the skin to swell.

❧

Colin screaming. I wake up at night and feel the room closing
around me like the vise my father keeps in the garage. I think
it will break my skull. I sit with my blankets pulled up around
my shoulders and in the air all around me hangs Colin's scream.

❧

Frances asks me if I want to play. I look at her; we are standing
by the chain-link fence that surrounds the yard, locks us into
recess. Her blonde hair is pulled into a ponytail so tight that her
eyes bulge slightly. A few feet away her friends are waiting,
scuffing their feet. This is more than an invitation; it's an
endorsement. I can play with Frances publicly. I can be seen,
playing. Frances waits, pulling at her ponytail. Get real, I want
to tell her. I've got better things to do. I look at Frances, at her
watery blue eyes. Wipe your nose, Frances, I want to say, let
your hair down. I glance around for Magdelene, but I don't
know where she's gone. A soft wind touches my forehead,
strokes my face. I look at Frances's friends, fidgeting by the
fence. "Okay," I say. "I'll play."

❧

When I come home from school something is wrong. My
mother is in her chair at the table, her head in her hands. I think
at first that she is sleeping, but then I see her shoulders shaking.
She is alone in the room with the afternoon sun and she is
crying as if she will never stop, her head buried now in her
arms. I want her to tell me why. Her crying frightens me, fills
my chest with a lump that trembles until I am shaking, too. I go

to her, touch her, and she pulls me into her lap, strokes my hair, and for a moment it is the way it used to be, when she used to hold me in her lap and read me stories.

For a moment I sink into her lap and think that everything will be all right, that things are back to normal, that I can be held like this again, and then I see the newspaper, folded open to the Deaths; I see Dan's face, grainy in the newsprint. Black and white; his eyes without color. I don't know what to say. I only sit there in her lap and run my fingers around the rim of her chair. The pattern on the cushion there has faded over the years, the fabric so worn I can almost see through it.

I sit and trace with my finger the chair's flowers and swirls, some still bearing faint traces of color. Dan is smiling in his picture, smiling beneath his Marine Corps hat. The wood of the armrests has been worn to a shiny smoothness. *This can't be Maura, this can't be her.* This chair is so faded, the pattern is almost indiscernible. I look at his face in the picture, so smooth and relaxed, think of him touching the horn as he pulled out of the driveway the day he left with Colin. *This can't be Maura.* Green eyes. Green as Magdelene's. His hands reaching for the ball. My mother is crying again; she holds the paper so that I can't see it anymore. "I can't tell Colin," she says. "I can't tell him." I stay in her lap, keep myself as small as I can so that she won't remember I am here, won't tell me I'm too big for this, and all around us the sunlight streams into the room, touching our hair, our faces, touching Dan's face in the photograph, lighting his eyes.

⟡

The water in the creek is rapid with melted snow; it eddies and swirls and races for the rocks before the waterfall. I stand on the bank and press my cheek against a tree, wrap my arms around it. Dan takes the basketball, dribbles away from the net, turns to shoot. Colin's eyes watching him are blue in the sunlight, his hair yellow across his forehead. Dan's arms as he prepares to shoot are ruddy with sunshine, muscular and haloed with hair. He is alive, absolutely alive, and Colin, watching him take his shot, is alive as well. It is only my own aliveness that I cannot see, sitting off to one side, lost in the shade of the garage.

Colin calls that night from Vietnam, as if on cue. "I was just thinking of you," he says when I answer the phone. "All of a sudden," he says, "I just couldn't stop thinking of you."

When I hear his voice I don't know what to say to him, so I just keep quiet and let him talk, and he talks and talks, and I sit there on my mother's green bedspread and listen to his voice and all I can think is that Colin doesn't know, he has no idea that Dan has been killed. He has called just to say hello, and my mother will have to tell him that Dan is dead in some other part of Vietnam, that they won't be coming home together, and I sit here knowing that someone will have to say this to him. I am the first one to talk to him and I am not conscious of anything he says — I only sit there on the edge of my mother's bed with the receiver in my hand and think: He's in another country, and there's a war going on, and he's making conversation, and Dan is dead and he doesn't even know it.

My mother comes into the room, with her yellow bathrobe belted tight around her waist, and takes the phone out of my hand. I am glad when she takes it, because I can't stand it anymore, just sitting there making conversation. I feel dishonest making bright and shiny conversation when this evil lurks on the line. My mother takes the phone and sits down on the bed and motions me away, and when I get to the doorway I look back and she has the phone against her face and she is trying to tell him straight out, and then her hands are shaking, her shoulders are shaking, and all she can say is "Dan," and standing there in her doorway, I see that the whole room is soft with the light of the lamps on her dresser. She sits there on her bed clutching her yellow bathrobe around her and her shoulders are shaking and I think of Colin alone in a phone booth some- where, hearing the news, and I wonder if it's raining there or if the night is clear, and what he sees through the glass of his booth while he hears the thing my mother tells him. I know only that my mother is sitting on her bed, trying to tell him the news, and there is something in her grip on the receiver, in the way her fingers hold her yellow bathrobe to her throat, that seems to take and wring out all the darkness and all the evil that is there on the line. Something about her telling him lays it to rest, and somewhere on the other end Colin is hanging up the phone.

Colin puts his head against my chest. I wrap my arms around him, hold him to me. We sit in silence, me just holding him, holding his head against my chest, and I think that this is all I want, this is all that I will ever want, just to sit here just like this with Colin, and then I see the gun in his hand, I see him lift it, and it is like a dream in which I have no voice. Colin, I want to say, Colin, stop — but I cannot remember his name, he has been gone so long, and I say nothing, *nothing,* as he lifts the gun to his head and pulls the trigger, and in the explosion that follows I find my voice and his name and scream it, again and again as his head breaks open in my arms, as bits of his brain matter splatter my face, and the sound of his name hangs in the air as his body goes slack in my arms and the sound of the gun fades away. There is only my screaming, out of control, as I try to gather what is left of Colin in my hands.

The next day in school, the girls are taunting Betsy Gleason. She's at this school on scholarship. She wears our cast-off clothes at home; her hair hangs in strings about her face. She crouches where they have chased her, in one corner of the playground; she cowers almost on her knees, her hands flung up, palms outward, to shield her face, while the girls surround her, standing arm in arm like troopers, shouting at her, shouting accusations.

I hear them from my corner, where I am leaning up against the fence, and I walk over to them. Frances sees me coming and waves me over; her braids are flying in the breeze. "Maura," she calls. "Come here."

I walk over to the ring they have formed around Betsy. I don't even wait to hear what they are saying; I walk right into their midst and with my right hand I take hold of Betsy's shoulder and push her down into the dirt. I seize hold of her and push her down and I do not even know the crime with which she's charged. I stand there for a moment and watch her scramble to her feet, her eyes avoiding mine and her face streaked with dust, and feel something deep in my stomach clench like a fist. Betsy is rubbing her nose with one hand, rubbing away her tears and snot, and when I look at Frances and the other girls they are not paying any attention to me; they are still yelling at Betsy. I back away from them and feel this thing in my gut that is not guilt or pride or any formed emotion, but only a pressure deep within me, a feeling I will carry with me for the rest of my life. That and the feeling of my hand on Betsy's shoulder, pushing her down. That vision of Betsy, scrambling to her feet, scrambling away from me, her eyes focused on the ground, avoiding mine.

I look around me as I leave, but Magdelene is nowhere in sight. No one has seen it, what I have done.

My mother and I are in the parking lot of the supermarket and she is handing the bags to me as I arrange them in the backseat of the car. I am taking the last bag from her when we see Dan's parents walking in our direction. My mother straightens up; one hand touches her hair, smooths it back. His parents do not look at us, just walk right past; they look years older than my mother, loading their groceries into the trunk of their car. Dan's mother is all stooped over opening the door. His father is tall and thin and looks like Dan, but with folds all through his face. He helps Dan's mother into the car and then he gets into the driver's side, shuts the door. He does not look at my mother. He does not look at me. He only starts the car and pulls out of the space, while beside me my mother still pats at her hair, even though it's all in place.

My mother slams the cupboard door shut on the cans she's put inside, then turns around and opens another cupboard and begins rearranging groceries she's already put away. "But Colin went," she says to my father, who stands in the doorway, watching her. "He's over there now, he went over *with* Dan," she says. "Doesn't that count for anything?" She slams the door shut and puts her hand against her mouth. Her cheeks are streaked with tears, which soak through the powder to track the wrinkles underneath. My father doesn't answer her, just turns and walks away, heading for the basement door. She asks if it still counts, but I know, even then, even now, that nothing counts for anything anymore.

The nights are long while Colin is gone. Adele sleeps out in the barn, curled up in the straw next to Colin's dog, while I sit by the fire and draw pictures with my colored pencils until my mother makes me go to bed. I draw the flames spitting out the chunks of burning ash that my father sweeps into a pan and throws back in. I draw Colin, holding my hand in the woods while we walk.

Magdelene catches my eye across the classroom and winks. It's question-and-answer time in religion class; Sister Rosaria is letting us ask about God, Jesus, the saints, whatever we want to talk about. She is so generous in her offer that I wonder if this is not an institution, like confession or communion — doubt time. Magdelene looks at me and rolls her eyes. I slouch at my desk and look at the floor. I wonder what Magdelene would say if she knew about Betsy. I wonder if Magdelene would like me if she really knew me.

In the front of the room, Sister Rosaria waits for us to talk. I wonder what she would say if I told her that God had died in me, but I keep my mouth shut; instead, I sit and trace faces into my notebook. Across the aisle Frances raises her hand. She has a question. It figures. Frances is such a suck-up. Her knees stick out when she stands up; they look like praying mantis heads. Her blouse is flat across her chest. She has a mouth like a grape, round and slightly green around the lips; the nuns adore her. They adore the flatness of her chest: the buttonholes never stretch, a danger even in the seventh grade, one that sometimes necessitates conversations with parents that the nuns would prefer not to have. The nuns carry a tape measure around with them to measure our skirts. They whip it out at odd moments, to catch us when we're unawares — "No more than an inch above the knees, girls," they say, smiling falsely. Frances has hers down to the quarter inch.

Frances stands now with one hand lightly touching the top of her desk as if to support herself. "Sister Rosaria," she says softly, her voice low and breathless. Since when did she become so fragile? "Sister Rosaria, what should we do with a holy statue when it breaks?"

I steal a look at her: surely she can't be serious. Her face is smooth and solemn, her lips pucker around her words, and her hair lies flat in braids. She stands when she talks; I never stand. Though it is not specifically forbidden by my mother, I put it in the same category as kneeling during Mass.

At the front of the class, Sister Rosaria looks like a cow, her mouth moving constantly, just a little, as if she's feeding on her tongue. She holds her chalk in the palm of her hand, watching Frances with her dimpled cheeks. Sister Rosaria's voice is high and flat, thin like the shallow water that trickles through the creek in the woods in summer.

"You must bury it," she says. Her voice trembles just a little. "You mustn't throw it in the garbage. It must be buried."

Oh, give me a break, I think. We pay for this? I glance at the clock on the wall. The bell is about to ring, but across the room Magdelene raises her hand. For a moment I think that Sister Rosaria won't call on her, but she does, with obvious reluctance. Magdelene lets her words tremble, just a little, and drift across the rows of chairs to where Sister Rosaria stands like a bird on a wire, waiting. "I always wondered," Magdelene says, slowly, "if the Virgin Mary didn't just make the whole thing up, to tell her mother..."

The bell rings before Sister Rosaria can recover. We all file out for recess. Magdelene heads for her secret corner, her hand already reaching into her pocket for her cigarettes. I start to follow her, but Frances and her entourage get there first.

"What do you think you're doing?" Frances hisses. She sounds like she's missing teeth.

Magdelene looks at her with one eyebrow raised and one foot pressed against the wall for balance, cups her hand around her cigarette, and lights it. Her cheeks go gaunt as she inhales. She looks like a Madonna. She takes the cigarette out of her mouth and exhales, right at Frances. "What do you mean?" she asks.

Frances backs away from the smoke, losing ground. "Magdelene," she says, looking around at her friends for support. "Magdelene the whore," she says. Frances is so inarticulate; she can't carry any argument through without resorting to one-liners.

Magdelene straightens up, grinds her cigarette out on the wall. "The whore," she says, taking a step toward Frances. "I wonder," she says. "Do you even know what that means, Frances?"

Frances is backing up; she's looking for her friends. "Slut," she says, her voice faltering a little.

Magdelene steps closer to her. "Really?" she says. "How do you know?" She is nearly touching Frances now. "How do you know?"

Frances is shaking; she looks like she might cry. "Leave me alone," she says, uncertainly.

"You started this," Magdelene says. She reaches out, picks up one of Frances's braids, and holds it in her hand, strokes it with her fingers. "Who's the slut?" she whispers.

The tears in Frances's eyes spill over. For a moment I almost feel sorry for her. "Leave me alone," she says, but her voice is small and thin. A sob tears at her throat. She turns around, bumps into her friends. "Leave me alone," she says, again, and pushes through them, stumbling to the front door, rubbing her eyes with her fists.

Magdelene reaches back into her pocket, extracts another cigarette. She looks at me and winks. "Crybaby," she says, lighting it. The other girls exchange glances, start to break away in clumps. Frances is standing by the door, praying for the bell to ring.

🐦

Beyond the basketball hoop on the wall of the garage is the field that leads down to the woods. It is a field I run through every day after school, pushing my feet into the earth and forcing myself forward until I feel the effort in my chest, digging my toes into the earth and pushing off, knowing that if I push hard enough, I can fly; if I thrust my body off this ground with enough concentration, with enough intention, I can fly, I can take off before the open mouth of the woods takes me in, I can take off and leave the trees beneath me, I can leave it all beneath me, all of them, all of them in their uniforms and their knobby knees and their stupid regulation knee socks, if I just try hard enough — I run and the woods open to take me in and close behind me, and I am left in a darkness as warm and as wet as the press of my tongue against my teeth.

🐦

Davey Janeski invites me to his house after school. He doesn't have to ride a bus; he lives close enough to walk, and he makes me walk ten paces behind him until we are out of sight of the schoolyard. Then he lets me walk beside him, and when we get to his house his mother gives us cookies and milk and gives me one of Davey's older brother's sweatshirts and a pair of jeans so that we can go walking in the woods together. We walk far from his house, down by his creek, and when we get there the sun is setting and the water is clear and the air in the woods is tinged with the smell of pine needles. Davey Janeski turns to me and puts a timid hand on my shoulder and I don't even let him try to make the first move: I pull his face to mine with both hands and fit my lips to his and it seems like the easiest thing in the world, to be kissing Davey Janeski down by his creek with the sun setting all around us and me in his older brother's sweatshirt. Before we go back, Davey asks me for my pocketknife and I give it to him without hesitation, but then I see that he is going to carve our initials into the bark of the tree beside us, and I think of Colin's admonition and I start to object and then I stop, and just watch him carve out our names and enclose them with a heart, and when he turns to me again I only let him touch my face and press his lips to mine, but beneath it is a sense of guilt — I have betrayed Colin twice, first by giving away the stone, and then by letting someone kill a tree. I close my eyes to put his image from me, and hug Davey Janeski with the entire length of my body.

🐍

At night the air drifts in through the open window and the curtains wave in the breeze and somewhere Colin is running for cover, diving beneath the bush. Colin's body hurling itself through the air like a bullet, all around him screams, the sound of gunfire, Colin who is so small and pale and light he can ride on the air, while the ground beneath him leaps into flame.

🐍

The Sunday papers are filled with pictures that I rip out without knowing why when my mother asks me. Children with stumps of arms propped up on crutches or teeth rotting in open mouths, the twisted shoulders of a little girl lying on the side of a hill with her head bent back until her throat curves upward like an offering. Her eyes are open; I stare at them and they are dark, her hair is dark; she looks like me. She looks just about my age. I turn the picture upside down and her eyes look at me like she's still alive. I hold her eyes between my hands and I think: She is dead. She is my age and she is dead and her eyes looking at me when this picture was taken are dead. I do not know who killed her. I do not understand what is happening to the world. The pictures I have torn from the page lie scattered on the dinner table between my mother's candleholders like bodies. I gather them in my hands and take them upstairs to my room. I lay the pictures out on my bed and I look again at the eyes of the girl my age. I look around my room, at all my familiar things, my books and my desk and my writing paper, my drawing pad and my window that overlooks the driveway, and I wonder if, wherever Colin is, he's seen her, too.

The nuns tell us stories of people coming back from the dead, bearing messages. Sister Rosaria leans toward us across her desk and speaks softly, as if taking us into her confidence. "I had an aunt," she says, "whose cousin died when she was little. They had her in the front room while she was ill so that they could take care of her, and one night my aunt was sitting on the front porch, on the porch swing, and it was a dark and windy night and all around the house the trees were blowing, and suddenly she saw a man dressed all in black coming out of the shadows, and he walked toward her, very slowly, and didn't even pause when he reached her, just came up the porch steps and on into the house without even glancing at her, and after a minute or so he came back out, closing the front door behind him and walking back down the steps with never a backward glance, and dissolved back into the shadows cast by the trees in the wind, and at that moment there came a scream from inside the house, and my aunt ran inside and her cousin's mother was screaming, on her knees beside the bed, her child in her arms, screaming, *'She's dead, my baby's dead,'* and all around them the shutters were banging against the house in the wind and above all that noise the sound of the mother's scream kept splitting the air like an ax."

The stories are endless; the nuns never run out of them; their supply is as bottomless as their collection of suffering saints. I sit at my desk and keep silent, motionless. There are no ghosts in my religion. My mother gets impatient with me when I try to repeat these stories to her, so I stop, but at night when I'm alone in my end of the house I am afraid to look behind the shower curtain in the bathroom, afraid to look behind closed doors, afraid to turn out the light before I sleep, afraid to roll over in my bed for fear there'll be somebody there. I am afraid to look out of my window into the darkness for fear of what might emerge — the angel of death stalking our house, looking for Colin; Dan, walking up to the house with his duffel bag in his hand, his hair cut so short that his scalp shows. I am terrified of seeing him now, of seeing the thing he has become, now that his soul has been taken from him. I lie stiff in my bed with my fists closed until the sun has risen and it is safe to open my eyes.

❧

I find Colin's dog out in the barn one night when I take her food out to her. She is stretched out, silent, her sides not moving. Her eyes are open, fixed on the wall. I poke her gently with my finger. She doesn't move. I stare at her for a while. Where has she gone? My father buries her out back behind the garage and for a while I go back there and look at her grave with Adele, wonder if she's anywhere around. If she is, Adele doesn't seem to notice, just sniffs around the trees, waiting for me to take her to the woods.

❧

I walk through the woods with Adele when school is over and I do not have to help my mother in the kitchen. I skip stones along the creek, jam my hands deep into my pockets, stand motionless beneath the trees with my eyes closed while Adele searches the underbrush for squirrels. I play a game with myself to see how long I can stand without moving, without opening my eyes, entombed beneath the trees, breathing the air so lightly that my nostrils do not move. I get a rush from doing this, the same rush I imagine comes with death. Alone, immobile, I play dead with myself beneath the trees.

I barely listen anymore to what the nuns say in school. I only sit and occupy a space. I know how to look attentive while my mind is far away, back in the woods, somewhere in the fields, flying through the clouds. I just sit in my seat, exchange a look now and then with Magdelene across the room, and wait for recess, when we can go off into our corner of the yard and fill our lungs with nicotine. The nuns no longer call on me, no longer aim remarks in my direction. School is like a blanket smoothed across a bed, everything so level you'd think that nothing had happened. I pull myself into my head and no longer pay attention. I no longer know what it is that I'm supposed to be.

The school year is nearly over. The days already feel like summer; the air is electric with warmth, intoxicated with its own sudden power. I'm not excited anymore by the change. I'm bored at home, playing the same old games with myself, with Adele the same old audience. I wander through the fields after school, hike the trails in the woods, look for flowers and robins.

I swing on the gate in the pasture. The pasture holds nothing but weeds and wildflowers now, a pen of wild grass that is higher than my head. I swing on the gate and pretend that it's a horse. Straddling the gate with both hands on the wood, I push off with my foot and let the gate carry me back and forth. I sit straight up and close my eyes and let the wind blow in my face and the sun burn my skin, pretending I'm on a horse. No.

I pretend to pretend. I know it's not a horse. I know it's only wood. I'm too old for these games now. I can't deceive myself anymore.

I walk through the pasture and into the woods; I cut through the trees and down toward the waterfall. The path leads down into what used to be a quarry: smooth stone slabs stretch high above my head. A thick stone bridge extends halfway across the creek and stops in midair. Below, the rubble from its collapse has long since been swept away. A handrail starts along its side and then stops. I run my hand along it to its end and there are not even any splinters left. I stand on half a bridge and below me is the waterfall, surging down rock gone flat with age, surging and foaming and coursing on beneath me. I stand poised above the water, one hand on a rail that leads nowhere.

eight

September 1971

Colin comes home from Vietnam the fall I enter the eighth grade. He comes home as he left it, in the middle of the night. I am lying in bed, absolutely motionless, the covers pulled up to my chin. The night outside is black and silent, starless, and I think I am the only one awake in the entire world. I lie without moving and through the window that is open just a little for air I think I hear a footfall. I lie without moving and I hear it again. I push the covers back and sit up, afraid to breathe, afraid to look outside, but the footsteps are unignorable now, coming one after another up the driveway.

I push back the curtain and look out. Colin is walking up the driveway, his duffel bag in his hand and his dark blond hair cut short, and when he reaches the front steps he stops walking, just stands there, still, looking at the house, and in the moment that his eyes reach my window, the lights go on in my parents' room and his eyes close in their glare. His hand tightens on his bag and his face goes masklike, and through the night air I hear my mother's cry.

❧

My mother cries when she sees him; I hang back by the doorway and just look at him. There seems a huge distance between us — much larger now than when he was actually away. In his absence he seemed taller to me, tall and gold and strong, but here in this hallway with my mother's arms around him and her head pushed into his chest, he looks awkward: his too-short hair reveals the acne around his hairline, he is patting my mother's shoulder distractedly with one hand, and I know that he is looking for my father. "It's okay, Mom," he whispers, and gently takes her arms away.

He goes into the kitchen and my father is leaning against the sink, not looking at him. "Hi, Dad," Colin says, and sticks his hand out toward my father. My father takes his hand and shakes it; I stand in the doorway and it is ludicrous somehow, my father just shaking his hand when his eyes are all loose and watery. He looks so old, my father does; he stands there shaking Colin's hand and suddenly I see him standing in this kitchen he has paced so many nights and he looks old. My mother, standing on tiptoe with her hand on Colin's arm, doesn't look half so old; her eyes are wet too, but her face is shining from it, all pink and white and soft, while my father stands there holding Colin's hand like he can't let go and he doesn't say a word, and neither does Colin.

❧

I take his bag upstairs for him, lay it on his bed, the single twin bed with its pale plaid blanket stretched tight across it, free of wrinkles. I lay the bag down and for a moment we just stand there together, neither of us speaking, beside that second-story window overlooking the maple trees that front the house. Outside a gentle early-morning wind has begun to blow, lifting the branches of those ancient maples, dying now, whose roots have filled the ground beneath the surface of our yard. They stand there now, slightly stooped, slowly, silently suffocating for lack of room, and inside Colin and I stand silent beside his flat twin bed, not knowing what to say.

❧

When I wake up the next morning, it feels like Christmas. At first I can't think why, and then I remember that Colin has come home. I push back my covers and run down the hallway to his room, but he is already up. His bed doesn't even look slept in.

I run downstairs and into the kitchen. My father is getting himself a cup of coffee at the counter beside the sink. He is peering through the window. "Looks like it might rain," he says. He takes a sip of his coffee, winces like it hurts him.

My mother is sitting in her chair at the table, reading the paper. She glances up when she sees me. "Good morning," she says.

I look around me. You'd think that nothing had happened; for a moment I wonder if I dreamed the whole thing, but then I hear Colin's whistle outside, Colin's step on the front walk. I throw open the front door, run outside, and throw my arms around him. "Hi, Colin," I say, burying my head against his chest. "Welcome home," I say, and look up at his face.

He's not looking at me; he's staring at the house, one hand patting my shoulder distractedly. "Of course," he says. "No problem." His voice is bright and full of a cheer that sounds hollow. His eyes look out of focus to me. "I'll get right on it," he says.

I want to shake him, suddenly; instead, I find myself backing away, still staring at him. "Colin?" I say. I wonder for a moment who this man is. He doesn't even look like Colin. There are lines in his face that were never there before. One corner of his mouth sags, and his shoulders are stooped. He looks like he might duck at any moment. "Hey, Colin," I say, and he glances down at me as if he'd forgotten I was there. "I missed you," I say. Suddenly angry, I wonder if he remembers me.

For a moment Colin's eyes search my face and I think I see him in there, pondering, and then he goes back to staring at the house. "That's great," he says. "Just great."

I stand there and stare at him, and then I hear my mother at the door behind me. "Maura," she says. "It's time to get ready for school."

🍂

"Maura? I hear your brother's back. How is he?" I turn and see Sister Martha's face, peering into mine, the old familiar hairs along her jawline, the pinched skin where her face fades back into her habit. "Maura?" In her right hand she holds her measuring tape. "How is he doing?"

I study her, her yellowed skin, her graying teeth. Her colorless eyes. And for a moment there is a look almost of real concern within her eyes, for a moment her face is almost gentle, but I will not let this happen, I will not permit myself to see it.

"He's fine," I say, "just fine." And then I turn and walk away, leaving her with the measuring tape hanging from her fingers, the flesh of her face sagging along its bones.

Magdelene falls in step with me, lightly punches my arm. "Hey," she says. "What's up?"

I walk along beside her. I feel like I'm underwater, like we'll never make it to the school building. I don't answer, but she seems to understand. She puts her arm around me as we walk.

❖

I watch Colin where he sits in his chair by the fire. His hair is still so short, butchered up over his ears, that his scalp shows through it, here and there. I sit opposite him on the floor beside the fire and burn my paper dolls in the flames: I make them houses out of Kleenex boxes, cut out windows and paste my people into them, set the houses on the logs and watch my people burn to death, shriveling silently within their cardboard prisons. I look at Colin sitting across from me and I want to talk to him; I want to ask him questions. I sit there and I look at him rocking in his chair, picking at the fringes on the blanket, and I wonder what he's thinking. "Colin?" I say, but he doesn't answer me. He just sits there and he rocks and his eyes look at nothing. I watch the flames turning the edges of arms brown on the log.

I go into the kitchen, where my mother is, and watch her dicing onions on her cutting board. Around her forehead her hair is curling a little, from the heat. Her face is dark with concentration, dark in the shadows of the room.

"What's the matter with Colin?" I ask her. "Why won't he talk to me?"

My mother doesn't look at me, just takes the onions over to the stove and sweeps them from the cutting board into the pot of soup warming on the back burner. "Give him time," she says.

"What did he do in Vietnam?" I ask her. I follow her over to the stove, hand her the wooden spoon from the counter when I see that she is hunting for it, slamming drawers in and out like she doesn't know where anything is in here anymore.

"He served his country," my mother says, dipping her spoon into the pot, stirring the soup for our dinner. "Just let it rest," she says, turning to me, wiping her hands on her apron, pushing those curls back from her forehead. "Leave him alone," she says, and walks around me to the icebox; I am conscious of the air between us when she passes me. I think she does not want to touch me. "Just keep quiet about it," she says, taking a bag of carrots from the icebox and dumping it on the counter.

I take a carrot from her cutting board and leave the kitchen, go back into the living room. I sit across from Colin by the fire, chew my carrot in silence, throw my families into the flames. My paper people curl up brown before they die.

I come home from school and Colin is lying on the blanket on his bed. I have run up the stairs to see him; I hang in the doorway, panting. "Colin?" I say. My heart is hammering against my chest. "Come take a walk with me," I say. Colin doesn't answer me, just lies there with his arms folded beneath his head, staring at the ceiling. His room is neat, barracks-style neat. It does not look as if he lives there. There is nothing in the room that connects me to Colin. Beside the bed his dresser stands with nothing on top of it — no loose change, no mirror, no hairbrush. No dust. Beside it is his desk, the chair pushed in as if he has never sat in it. On the desk is a calendar pad — nothing else, no pens, no paper. The bookshelf on the other side of his bed stands untouched. The rug lies squarely in the center of the room. There is nothing in the room that lets me know he lives there, except for him, lying stretched out on his back, motionless.

"Colin?" I say. "Do you want to take a walk?" If he hears me, he gives no clue. His eyes stare straight ahead; his face is empty of expression. I stand looking at him where he lies, immobile, on his blanket, and I think I cannot bear it. I stand there in the doorway and something starts to build in me, as if my heart were trembling, the way the earth moves just before a quake. I look at Colin and I want to shake him, I want to hit him, I want to take hold of his shoulders and jerk him up, make him look at me. I want his face to change. I want him to look at me. I want his eyes to focus. I want him back. I think that Zach would never look like this. Zach would meet my eyes. Zach would never give up. Zach would never just lie there, staring at nothing I can see.

I stand there in the doorway of Colin's room and I want my brother back, but my mother has told me not to bother him. She has told me to leave him alone, to give him time. I don't want to give him time. He has had enough time away from me.

"Colin?" I say, but he doesn't answer me. There is so little movement in the room it is like a graveyard. As I turn to leave, I see the calendar pad on top of his desk. No one has changed the date; it remains torn off at the month he left for Vietnam. "Colin," I whisper. "Come to the woods with me." Colin doesn't move; he lies there, corpselike, on his bed. I leave, walk downstairs alone, go outside alone.

❧

I walk in the woods by myself. Adele is nowhere to be found. The trees along the trail are on fire with leaves, blazing all up and down the hillsides, along the creek, within the glens. The woods are unfolding, opening up, turning a dozen shades of red and yellow. It is as if someone had taken a match to them; burning, the leaves tear themselves from their branches and float to the ground. Everything else is muted; dusk falls so slowly that the light touches every leaf before receding. "Name three things," I whisper to the leaves that flutter from the trees. The air is soft, gentle. There is no threat in the woods. We are all at peace amid these trees. We are all at peace because we are alone. I tell my stories to the trees, watching as their leaves fall, one by one, and leave them bare.

🍂

"What would you do if you knew you had one month to live?" Magdelene asks me. We are sitting on the floor of my room, assembling a project for social studies, a collage of inferior cultures oppressed by the Iron Curtain. We are smoking cigarettes with the door shut and all the windows open.

"I don't know," I say. I am cutting with my scissors around some old woman's face, concentrating on the lines. Her skin looks like parchment. My parents' *National Geographic* magazines lie around us, shredded. Nothing occurs to me to do with my final month.

"I'd drop out of school," Magdelene says, taking another draw on her cigarette. "I'd travel all around the world." She kicks the cut-up magazines, contemptuously. "I'd go to all these places," she says. "I'd see them all firsthand." Her eyes are bright with the thrill of it; they shine at me through the smoke in the room. "Come with me," she says, and touches my hand, takes my hand in hers.

"Okay," I say, looking at her eyes. Anything, I think. Just don't leave me here. Let's go now, I want to say. Let's make a break for it, climb out through these windows and let ourselves into the world. Let's blow this joint.

Magdelene takes her hand away, picks her scissors up again. "Hand me Hungary," she says.

🍂

At the dining room table my father sets his glass of beer down on his coaster with a thud that restores him to our consciousness.

"What the hell are you going to do with your life?" he says, and as he says it I become aware of Colin, sitting across the table from me, staring vacantly into his dinner. Magdelene, beside me, looks nonplused. This is the first time she's come home with me. Till now I've tried to avoid showing her my world.

"Well?" my father says. "What are your plans? You've been home for a month." Beside me my mother seems to shudder, then collects herself.

"Saul," she says, but my father will not heed her.

"Answer me," he says. "Goddammit, I'm talking to you."

Across the table Colin stirs, shakes his head as if to clear it, stops curling the placemat up around his plate. He looks a little sharper now, seems to be taking on some definition, as if my father's words have brought him into focus, brought him to life. He looks up, and for just a moment I think I see him in the blue of his eyes. Beside me, Magdelene doesn't move.

"Well?" my father says.

"Saul—" my mother breaks in, twisting her napkin.

"Let him answer," my father says — snarls, nearly.

My brother looks at him without speaking, hardly blinking, and his eyes are like the creek in the middle of winter, the color of the water when it freezes, with just a hint of movement beneath the surface.

"Colin," my mother says. "Do you want to go to college?"

For a moment everything is so silent I think that something is about to break, something I sense gathering at my father's end of the table.

"Your veteran's compensation should pay," my mother says, "and if you do—"

"Oh, great," my father says, "he can go to college and end up like Zachary, with communist professors filling his head with bullshit—"

He says this and something clicks in my head: I see Colin on his knees before the fireplace, burning college catalogues; I see Colin's eyes, in the light of the fire, red and swollen and full of tears; I see Colin as he was before, when I knew him, when he walked with me; and before I know what I am doing I turn to my father and the voice that comes from me is a snarl like his.

I do not remember having heard this sound coming from my mouth before.

"It's a little late, isn't it," I hear my voice say, "for him to end up like Zachary — don't you think?"

In the pause that follows I see the surprise in my father's eyes; it is there for just a moment, before his brows come together. "Maura," my mother says, but her admonition comes too late; my father's hand is up and with a crack it snaps across my face, so that the sound of it is with me longer than the sting. I see Magdelene wince, and for a second I think it's Magdelene who's been struck.

Across the table Colin gathers himself up, the way I gather up my work at school when it's time to go home, gathers himself up like so many pens and pencils and takes himself away, as I sit, motionless, in my seat, touching my cheek, while at one end of the table my mother begins to cry and at the other my father pushes off from his chair and stamps to the front door; he is muttering to himself, and I do not recognize his words as he pushes open the door and disappears into the night. The door slams behind him like a gunshot before the silence falls on us, slowly, like the night, like an ending, until it takes us over, lulls us, until we sleep.

🖙

Colin goes to work at the bank on Water Street. He takes a teller job, walking the four miles into town every morning and back home each night. He takes up yoga, and at odd hours I find him standing on his shoulders in some corner of some room. He begins to cook for himself, without meat, and takes his meals alone in the kitchen after the dinner dishes have been done. My parents don't say anything about it. No one says anything, to anyone, about anything. We live our lives, get up, brush our teeth, go to work or to school, reconvene in the evening. I spend my time after dinner in my room, drawing pictures in my notebook, making paper-doll families, one after another, until I have no more space to keep them, until they seem to take up more room than I do, and then I stop. Outside, the leaves grow thick, the katydids begin to sing. The world goes on, and every day Colin does his job, and nobody says a thing about it.

❦

We have a new nun now, Sister Mary Fortitude; she tells us on her first day that we are going to do heritage this term. She is a tall, broad woman, like her name. We call her Sister Fort. She asks us where our families are from, starts a chart on the wall. Frances's family is Irish; she knows the county her great-grandparents came from, her grandmother's maiden name. Rosemarie is Sicilian; she has nine brothers and sisters, one born every year; the picture she brings in of her mother looks postmortem. Her grandfather and his brothers came here together; he still lives with them. Davey Janeski's family is Polish. I anguish as she nears my row. What will I tell her? I know my parents speak in German sometimes, late at night and not so much anymore, but beyond that I know nothing. No towns, no dates. The others all have cousins; I don't remember ever meeting any of my own. No other family member has ever been in our house.

Sister Fort is on me, tapping the pointer against her palm. "Yes, Maura?" she says. "Maura," she says again. "Was your mother Irish?" I glance at Frances. How Irish can I possibly look? My mother's name, I know, was Bauer, but before I can think of a response, I hear Chuckie Supulski's low hiss from the back of the room.

"Come on, Maura," he says. "Is it Canada or Vietnam?"

Sister Fort stiffens. Her knuckles go white on her pointer, her lips squeeze tight. "Young man," she says to Chuckie Supulski, "if someone in Maura's family has been to Vietnam, that is nothing to joke about. If a member of her family has fought in the war, that makes her a patriot — a true American."

Her mouth trembles as she talks. The words go shrill in her throat. She is young yet, younger than the others, and fairly new around here. I feel almost sorry for her. They must not have briefed her very well. Or perhaps they no longer thought it was important.

"Sister Mary Fortitude," says one of Chuckie Supulski's friends, and his voice is so low it is almost a whisper. "What if a member of her family dodged the draft and went to Canada? What does that make Maura? Still a patriot?"

There is silence in the classroom, a communal intake of breath. Sister Fortitude stands before me, her face a white gleam of shock. The whole class waits; I wait too, curious about her answer. I want to know if my newfound status can be ripped away so quickly. Sister Fortitude doesn't seem to know what to say. She looks at me, helplessly. For a moment I see clearly how little power she has, how little power they all have, really.

There is a rustle from Chuckie Supulski's end of the room. "She's a traitor, Sister Fortitude — isn't she?"

"Shut up," somebody says, uneasily. They are all uneasy. This has not come up in a long time. "Her other brother fought," somebody says.

Through it all I wait, silent, at my desk. I want someone to tell me what I am. I want to get it straight. Sister Fort is different from the rest of them: she's not from here. She's come from somewhere else. If anyone can tell me, she can. I wait, my eyes fixed on her, and then I see her falter. I see that she has no words for me. She does not know what to say.

There is a movement behind me: Magdelene has risen to her feet. The bell is just about to ring; her timing is, as always, impeccable. "For God's sake," she says, and no one corrects her blasphemy. "Lay off it," Magdelene says. She turns to Chuckie Supulski. I can see her lip curl. "Get over it," she says, her voice low and even, smooth as butter in her mouth. "You little prick," she says.

Davey Janeski speaks up from the back of the room. "She's German," he says. "Leave her alone."

Sister Fortitude grabs this like a lifeline. "Oh, really," she says, fixing her eyes on mine again. "And where in Germany is your family from?"

"I don't know," I tell her. As I say it, the bell rings, the chairs around me scrape back from the desks, kids rise en masse, and Sister Fortitude looks away from me. As she does I see what has not occurred to me before. Sister Fortitude doesn't know who I am, any more than anyone else does. It does not matter where the nuns come from — they are all equally at a loss. I am an enigma to all of them. Undefinable. Unclassifiable. And it is this, more than anything else, that makes me dangerous to them. It is this that makes me unacceptable. As I collect my books to leave, Sister Fortitude turns and takes the chart from the board. Exiting, I turn back one last time. She has folded the board and is stuffing it, as deeply as it will go, into the trash.

🖙

"Where in Germany are we from?" I ask my mother that night as we put away the dinner dishes.

She pauses, drying a dish with a towel. "My family was from Austria-Hungary," she says. "Your father's was from northern Germany." She puts the dish into the cupboard, closes the door.

"Where are they?" I ask her, turning on the faucet to wash the food into the trap. "What happened to them?"

"They disappeared," she tells me. "All of them. During the war." She doesn't look at me. "Your father was the only one to get away," she says. "He's the only one that's left."

"You don't know where they are?" I ask her, and my mother puts the dishcloth down and turns to face me, wiping her hands on her apron.

"They died in the camps," she says. "We did the best we could," she says, "to find them."

🖙

Walking in the woods with Adele, I try to picture Zachary walking with me. I picture him tall and dark, brown eyed, with a beard. I think he must be full of body, not thin like Colin. I think that there must be a substance to him, that his shoulders never slope within his jacket, that his eyes are never vacant. I think that Zachary and I must talk together, as we walk. I think that Zachary must really be something, to have gotten away from all of this.

❧

The school year is coming to an end. The trees in the woods are budding now, coming back to life, awakening from their long and dreamless sleep. Magdelene walks beside me through the woods; we hold hands while the spring wind warms our faces. Life is everywhere; beside every rock, beneath each leaf, the wildflowers tremble, hesitate, then make themselves known, crocuses and ivy and paper fern. Birds sing as the breeze around us sheds its chill and softens, gentles. The afternoon lasts longer, twilight becomes less threatening. Magdelene squeezes my hand.

We stop and lean against a tree beside the path. Magdelene lights a cigarette, offers one to me. I shake my head, just watch her light it, watch the familiar movement of her face and hands as she gets that first bit of smoke into her lungs. Her hair is soft in the breeze; loose, it hangs down her back in a kind of subdued wildness. Her lashes touch her cheek when she closes her eyes; the skin of her face is flawless, unblemished. She seems to be skipping adolescence entirely — no acne, no misery. She has been menstruating for so long it's old hat to her by now. I just started recently. My body is still thin as a board, curveless, dull.

"What are you thinking?" Magdelene asks, looking at me.

I can feel myself blush, caught unawares. I feel put on the spot, don't know how much time has passed. Magdelene keeps looking at me; I want to tell her to stop. My neck is so hot I feel feverish.

Magdelene takes a last draw on her cigarette and puts it out. "It's okay," she says, and leans toward me till her eyes are close to mine. "Don't worry," she says. "You don't have to tell me," and then her head is touching mine. I can feel her lips brush my forehead. My heart is on fire suddenly, beating in my chest till I'm afraid it might explode, consume us on the spot, consecrate us as we stand here, much too close together.

Magdelene pulls back and steps closer to me, takes my head in her hands. She is taller than I am. Her breasts bump my chest. I am suddenly afraid I might throw up. I close my eyes; she kisses them. I keep them closed, feel her lips touch my nose, my cheeks, and then my mouth. Her lips are like deliverance, like a blessing. Her lips touch mine and my mouth opens like a flower, presents itself to her. My tongue touches her teeth, slips past them and into the soft, velvet cavern of her mouth. She sucks me in; like smoke, she inhales me, holds me in her mouth, then lets me go. She takes my hands in hers, puts them on her breasts. "Touch me," she says, and her voice is so soft I can barely hear it. I respond automatically; this is like a memory: I know exactly what to do. I slip my hands beneath her blouse. Her nipples grow hard beneath my palms. "That's perfect," she says, and I wonder for a moment how she knows, but then I stop thinking at all, shut my mind like shutting a book, and before I know what I am doing, I am fumbling with the zipper on her jeans, and she is pulling her shirt off over her head.

Even now, when I think of spring, when I go outside and feel that first warm breeze, inhale that first soft scent of spring, I see Magdelene's body at thirteen, lying on the floor of the woods behind my parents' house, olive white against the soft black earth beneath her. I can still feel her body beneath my hands, the shock of the hair between her legs, the way my fingers fit between her thighs. I can still remember how easily it came to me, to know a woman's body with my tongue.

🙵

June 1972

The nuns are in a flutter; they wring their hands and swoop around in groups like feeding crows. It is our eighth-grade graduation, and they are preparing for our final procession into the gym. Behind me, Frances tugs at her dress, rearranges it around her hips. I look back at her; her thin blonde hair is pinned behind her ears, straggles down her back. She looks much the same as she did three years ago, when I first came to this school. Her nose is running a little, and she wipes it on the back of her hand. For a moment she looks innocent, a kid with a cold; for a moment I can feel what it is to be her, Frances O'Malley, nondescript, thin and bedraggled, still measuring with her fingers to make sure her skirt is the acceptable length; and for a moment I feel almost sorry for her, worrying today of all days about whether she meets the requirements. For a moment I almost want to turn to her, say something to her, but then the nuns have rounded us up and paired us off into lines and I march in next to Davey Janeski.

Magdelene is a few people ahead of me; she turns and glances back at me, giving me a wink that starts my heart again, catches my breath in my throat, and makes my stomach flip, like dropping in an elevator. I march next to Davey down the aisle past the row where my mother sits, and I keep my face looking straight ahead, one hand touching the band of the watch my mother's given me for graduation. When my name is called I walk to the front of the room and get my diploma, and when I turn I scan the rows to find my mother's face, and when I do I turn away, look back at my empty chair, fix on it, pretending, as I walk, that Zachary sits next to her, tall and broad and visible, one arm stretched out along the back of my mother's chair; pretending, for the length of time it takes me to get back to my chair, that she is not sitting there alone.

It is summertime and we are free of school and Magdelene has gone off to summer camp somewhere in New England. All the trees are full of green and the houses in town are clean and shining. Water Street looks as if it's been washed; the pavement sparkles beneath the sun and above our heads the sky is blue and bright and everyone in town seems young and happy. I catch Colin one night after he gets home from work, before he can even go into the house.

"Take a walk with me," I say to him. I think for a moment that I will not be able to stand it if he doesn't. Please, I think to myself. Please say yes. I wait for his answer, wait to see if I have reached him. I have never been so lonely.

He hesitates, looks down at me as if he were trying to place me, and then shrugs. "Okay," he says.

I take his arm and lead him through the field, back toward the woods, where Adele catches up with us, falls in step. I reach Colin's shoulder now; I am as dark as he is pale. His dark blond hair hangs limp across his eyes. There is no color in his face. We walk through the woods with the summer sun still high in the sky and all the leaves neon green with its light. Now that I have him here beside me I can think of nothing to say. He walks along beside me, hands in his pockets, not looking at me, patient. "How are you?" I ask him, finally. I don't even know how to put what I want to know. "How is it," I ask him, "being back?"

We walk, and for a moment I think there is a falter in his step, one foot slightly misplaced, the barest flush across his cheeks. For just a second he seems real to me, he seems like the old Colin, who would take me by the hand and show me through the woods. For just a second, I think I have him back and I feel deep within me a rush of blood to my heart, and then he snaps together, catches himself before my eyes, turns to me, and smiles.

"Great," he says, "just great," and something in that smile shuts me up. "Just great," he says again, and, quickening his step, he turns up a path that will take us back to the field, nearly leaving me behind.

❧

My father's face is full of stubborn lines, creases between his eyes and around his mouth that have settled into his face over the years. His hair is thinning, and the scalp beneath it is spotted with brown. There is a perpetual twist to his lips, as if he were in pain. He is carving a pot roast that my mother has made for dinner. Colin is eating with us tonight; I don't know why. I don't know if I even care. All I want from these family dinners is to get through them, to get up to my room and be alone.

Colin clears his throat. My father stands there carving the meat with the same focused bitterness with which he does everything. "No meat for me, Dad," Colin says, and I can feel us all hold our breath at once.

There is a moment of silence before my father explodes. He lays down his knife and glares at Colin. "What are you," my father says, "some kind of fairy?"

My right hand tightens around my fork. I can feel myself begin to flush. "Dad—" I say.

"Shut up," he says, not taking his eyes off Colin. "What's the matter with you, boy," he says, "you some kind of queer?"

I can feel a pressure mounting in me; it starts in my stomach and moves up to my heart. I think I cannot breathe. For a moment I see Magdelene before my face, so close I almost smell her skin. I close my eyes, and take a breath. When I open them, Colin is sitting there smiling, his plate still extended for his food. There is something in that smile that ends dispute, because Colin isn't there anymore. Colin isn't in there. There is nothing in there behind that blue.

I look at my father all through dinner and I want to hurt him. The pot roast is dry in my mouth; it sticks in my throat when I try to swallow. I look at him and there is so much hatred in me that I think it will explode in me, explode and shatter my father like glass where he sits in his chair, drinking coffee. I want to tell Colin to stand up to him, I want to tell him not to take it, I want to tell him to stand up straight and lift his fist, and instead I am silent, and I see him roll inward, grip himself, and fall, never losing his smile.

❦

I just took it, after all, when I think back on it now. I just let him run right over me, too. It was so hard to talk to him. It was so hard to try to take him on.

Sometime in July my mother tells me I will not be going back to Catholic school in the fall. She tells me this early one morning while she is ironing. She does her ironing while the day is still cool, in one corner of the sewing room beside the open window. The ironing brings a flush to her cheeks, teases the hair around her hairline into little tendrils that curl around her brow. Her right arm is full of slender muscle; I think of all the things she does with it — the ironing, the sewing, the washing, the gardening. Her lips are pressed tightly together; her eyes focus on the sleeve of the shirt before her.

"We're going to send you to public high school," she says, finishing the sleeve and standing the iron up on its edge, folding the shirt into a square.

The air around me is suddenly lighter. A sentence has been lifted: I will not be going back to Catholic school. The whole world is different now. No one even seems to remember that the war is still going on. Nobody bad-mouths the draft dodgers anymore; they've been afforded a kind of prophet status. Maybe they weren't so stupid after all.

I am going to public school in the fall. There are so few chances for new beginnings. My mother irons, and I think what it will be to be someone no one knows. I will not be going back to Catholic school. The birds outside the windows sing and their song comes in through the curtains that rise and fall on the breeze. I am free. Freed of them. I leave my mother to her ironing and go outside, toward the woods, something in my chest expanding like the sky.

Only later, when I am deep in the woods, deep inside the trees, do I think of Magdelene.

nine

September 1972 "**P**ick a color," the freshman English teacher tells me.

I look at her uneasily. What does she mean, pick a color? What new tricks will I have to learn to survive in public school? She looks back at me, chalk in hand. She is young and slightly nervous-looking, with pale cheeks and long, dark hair pulled back from her face. It still seems strange to see a teacher's hair, to see her figure, to think of her as someone who has sex. Stop it, I tell myself. Just stop it.

Miss Greenway is still waiting, patiently. "Just pick a color," she says. "There's no right or wrong to it."

I take the first color that comes to mind. "Purple," I say.

Miss Greenway smiles. "Excellent choice," she says. Her smile implies that we share a secret. I'm not sure what it is. "Now take a walk," she says. It is early fall; the leaves outside the windows are still stubbornly green. I look at them with longing. Is she serious? I look back at her, but she has gone back to the class. "Everyone pick a color," she says, "and come take a walk with me."

We all get up, grab our notebooks, and file out of the room with her. "I want you to look for your color everywhere," she tells us. "And then I want you to write about it." She throws open the front doors, leads us outside, down the steps, out into the fresh air. The grounds around the high school are empty; for once there are no groups of kids smoking pot beneath the pine trees. I inhale, draw the fresh air deep into my lungs. I think I like this public school. The nuns would never encourage color sightings.

I look around me; the other kids from class are walking, too. They seem so much taller than the kids in Catholic school, so much older, without the saddle shoes and Peter Pan collars. The boys and girls dress alike, in jeans and sweatshirts, tennis shoes. No one looks any different from anyone else. They look more alike in their choice of dress than the kids in uniform. They have looks on their faces of concentrated boredom. No one shows any interest in me and this suits me fine. I walk and I breathe and I look for purple. I find it in the leaves, in the old cornstalks that cover the next field, in the clouds that trail across the sky, spindling down into nothing. I find it in Elizabeth's hair, in Jeannie's running shoes, in the belt that circles Miss Greenway's waist.

Back in the classroom, we write for fifteen minutes about our walk. "Don't worry about punctuation," Miss Greenway says. "Forget grammar." This is getting better and better. If this is public school, I can't imagine why I ever left. "Read yours," she says to me.

I can feel my heart begin to beat inside my chest, as if it comes to life only in times of stress, the rest of the time lying dormant, dry and shriveled. I make myself read my piece out loud. My throat feels parched. When I'm done I don't look up, wait for her to go on.

Nothing happens; I look up and she is just standing there, watching me. "Maura," she says, "is that your name?"

I nod; something seizes up in me. She's going to say it now; she's going to make some comment. This is when the measuring tape comes out. The atmosphere in the room turns to ice. The clock on the wall above the door freezes. Everything is absolutely still. I cannot breathe, for waiting.

"Maura," Miss Greenway says, as if she were tasting my name on her tongue. "That's beautiful," she says. "You write beautifully."

Something in me loosens; I want to cry. I stare at my notebook, feel a shaking in my chest that will not stop. I write beautifully. I cannot move when the bell rings. I cannot move until everyone else has left, gathered up their books and notebooks and left the room. Miss Greenway is watching me from her desk. "Where did you learn to write like that?" she asks. Her eyes on mine are large and brown, entirely without guile. Her face seems beatific to me. She is waiting for my answer, but I am suddenly on my feet, moving for the door like I'm afraid it will close and never let me out, leave me trapped in there with her, forced to account for the things I do.

❧

Colin has taken to running to work these days. He runs all the time now; he runs home from work and when he gets home he runs again. I see him stretching out in the basement in his shorts; his legs, raised above his head in a yoga pose in the corner of the room, are white and covered with hair, and through the window I watch their whiteness flash as he moves down the driveway toward the road. Colin runs for hours; I do not know how many miles he covers. I know only that when he is gone the house is still, except for my father, pacing back and forth from room to room, a beer in his hand, while my mother sews upstairs. My father paces, and from time to time he stops near the window as if he's trying to see beyond his own face in the glass.

❧

In history class I write a play about the French Revolution; my heroine makes impassioned speeches about Marat, putting her family in danger. One day the police arrive as she is speaking from a soapbox in the center of town. Her lover pushes her from view and the police arrest him in her place. She goes to watch him hang. I write this play sitting in front of the fireplace, my notebook on my knees. I write without stopping, not looking up until I am through. The teacher gives me an A. Miss Greenway gives me more and more assignments, gives me A's on all of them. It is the first time in years that my grades have been good. I have less and less time to walk in the woods now. The days are growing shorter again; I spend the evenings in my room, working at my desk beside the window. From time to time I put down my pen and look up, watch the sun as it sets into the woods at the bottom of the field. There seems to be nothing I can't say, once I pick up my pen to say it with.

❧

The telephone rings one night and it's for me. This almost never happens; I go to the phone in trepidation, not sure who it will be. The voice on the other end is like God's. "Hi, Maura," it says. It is Magdelene.

My heart comes back to life again. "Hi, Magdelene," I say.

"How are you?" she asks.

"Okay," I say, suddenly shy. We haven't talked since eighth-grade graduation.

"Do you want to come over?" she asks.

I think suddenly that there is nothing else I have ever really wanted. "When?" I say.

"What about Friday?" she asks me, and we make a date.

❧

Miss Greenway asks me to stay after class. I stand by her desk, wait for the kids to file out. When they are gone, the classroom is huge, open as a theatre. Miss Greenway is sitting on her desk, her legs crossed, her hands folded on her lap. She is wearing a green scarf knotted around her neck; she smells like the lilies of the valley that my mother grows. "Would you like to enter an essay contest?" she asks me.

I nod, wordless.

She hands me an information sheet, an entry blank. "The subject is friends," she says, and smiles at me. Her teeth are white and even; she has lips like Magdelene's, full and pink and soft-looking. "You've only got about a month," she tells me, and I nod again.

"Okay," I say, and head for the door.

"Maura," Miss Greenway says, and I look back at her. She looks like a picture, sitting there on her desk, leaning back on her hands, the sun coming in through the windows behind her. She could be a saint, the way the sunlight frames her head. "Show it to me before you send it off," she says. "I'll tell you what I think of it."

"Okay," I say, and curse myself. Why can't I think of something else to say?

"Good luck," she says, as I shut the door behind me.

On Friday night, I visit Magdelene. She is waiting for me on the front porch, waves to my mother as I get out of the car. Her parents aren't home, a fact I haven't told my mother.

"What's up?" Magdelene says.

"Not much," I say. Magdelene looks wonderful; her hair is tied back with a bandanna and she has on blue jeans and a red sweater I can see her breasts through.

"Come on," she says, and leads me upstairs to her room. The walls are covered with Grateful Dead posters. She has a black light and candles all around her bed. She lights some incense. "Sit down," she says, throwing some pillows on the floor. "You want to smoke some pot?" she says.

I have seen the kids doing this outside the public high school. They all wear ratty blue jeans and loose, shapeless shirts. Their smell is acrid. Magdelene opens the drawer of her dresser, pulls out a tightly rolled joint. "Have you done this yet?" she asks.

I shake my head. "It's cool," she says. "You'll like it." I cannot take my eyes off her. She looks kind of tired. Her skin is dark in the black light; her eyes stand out, like those of a ghost. She looks thinner than she used to. She puts the joint in her mouth and lights it. I remember our days of smoking cigarettes together, watching her suck in the smoke, and I feel a sudden longing, deep inside my stomach. She inhales and holds her breath, passes me the joint. I draw on it. It's not at all like cigarettes; the smoke rips right down into my lungs. I start to cough and Magdelene begins to laugh, and I suddenly remember my first cigarette in seventh grade. "You'll get used to it," Magdelene says, and I try again, inhale, hold the smoke in till I cannot bear it any longer, then let it out in a cloud that hangs in the air between us.

I pass the joint back over to her; her fingers brush mine as she takes it. My heart leaps in my chest. She inhales, passes it back. A sudden lightness floods my head, as if my worries have left it, as if my brain has left my body, left my heart at the helm.

It feels wonderful.

Magdelene smiles at me when I pass the joint back. "Keep it," she says. "I had some earlier." She reaches over, brushes my hair back from my face. "Your hair's getting longer," she says. She moves over closer to me, till we're sitting side by side against the pillows. She puts her arms around me, lays her head against my shoulder. I take another drag off the joint. I can't quite remember, suddenly, how long I've been here. Magdelene snuggles closer to me, touches my ear with her lips. "Call your mother," she whispers. "Ask her if you can spend the night."

Miss Greenway looks up from my essay. I straighten up eagerly, wait for her reaction. I spent all weekend writing it. Her face looks funny, like it can't decide between laughter and tears. "Have you shown this to anyone else?" she asks me.

I shake my head, feel sudden fear. Does she hate it, does the writing suck?

"I don't know," Miss Greenway says, carefully, "if this is exactly what they had in mind." She looks at me, touches my shoulder. Her hand is warm and gentle. I suddenly long for her to rub my back. "Maybe you should take out the sex," she says.

Magdelene and I visit every weekend, talk on the phone every night. We alternate whose house we stay at. We both prefer hers. "I think your dad is scary," she tells me, and I can't really argue with her. "And your brother..."

I look at her quickly.

"I'm sorry," she says. "I don't mean anything bad."

I know she doesn't. But I don't think that I can stand the thought of someone criticizing Colin.

🐦

I can't seem to finish the essay. I can't write about Magdelene without putting in the sex. I can't even think about Magdelene without thinking about her body naked, the way her breasts fall when she lies on her stomach, propped up on her elbows, reading a magazine to me while we lie in bed together, sharing a joint. Her parents are almost always out. We have the whole house to ourselves, but we seldom leave her room.

I put the essay away and turn off the light, climb into bed, and wait for sleep to come. When Magdelene stays here, she sleeps in the guest bedroom, Zach's old room, with the map on the wall that I imagine him plotting his escape to college on, all those years ago. We wait until the lights go off in my parents' room and then I creep down the hallway and slip into her room, close the door behind me. She'll be lying in the bed, the covers pulled up to her neck, her eyes nearly black in the darkness. "Hurry up!" she'll whisper, and then start to giggle. I'll have to run across the room and get in bed with her fast, put my hand across her mouth to stifle her laughter, and keep it there while with my other hand I touch her body everywhere, learning all her curves and planes. This seems like such a sacrilege, having sex in Zachary's room like this, amid all of his memories.

I think of this while I touch myself, while I slide my fingers down my own body, across my stomach, into the space between my own legs. I am learning to know myself as well. I think of Magdelene's tongue, licking my palm till her mouth tastes of salt when I kiss her. I think of Magdelene. I think of friends. I write draft after draft after draft. I can't think of her without thinking of sex.

❧

I take the drafts in to Miss Greenway. She reads them with a little furrow in her brow, glances up at me now and then, and then goes back to reading. Finally she looks up, touches my hand for a second, and smiles. "Never mind the essay contest," she says. "This is journal writing." She gets up, walks over to the window like she's thinking of something else. The sun strokes her hair, infuses it with light. She looks back at me. "Write for yourself," she says. "Don't take anything out." She gives me back the drafts. Her smile is a gift; what she says is a gift. "Fill notebooks," she says. "Just write. Be as true as you want."

❧

The next time I'm at Magdelene's, she doesn't have any pot. "Where do you get it, anyway?" I ask.

Magdelene smiles at me from where she is rummaging through her desk drawers. "From friends," she says. She goes to a Catholic high school in the city. I wonder suddenly how many friends she has. "Here it is," she says, pulling something out of one of the drawers. She turns to me and smiles. "I've got something else," she says. In her hand she has a bag of something, and what looks like a spoon. She takes a candle from the dresser and brings it over to me. "Wait'll you try this," she says, and I see that she has a needle in her hand.

I shake my head; this makes me uneasy. "I don't think so," I say. "I don't like shots."

Magdelene smiles at me. "This is nothing like a shot," she says. "You won't even feel this." She sits down, dumps the stuff between her legs, lights the candle. "Come on," she says, and her eyes on mine are as green as the creek water sometimes is, as green as the paper that I write on in my notebooks. I start to shake my head again, but then the room lights up. A car has pulled into the driveway. Magdelene runs to the window, peeks out from behind the curtain. "Shit," she says. "My parents are home."

We scoop everything up, dump it back into the drawer. Magdelene's starting to shake. "Go down and talk to them," she says, "before they come up here."

"What do you mean?" I say. I don't want to talk to her parents. We hear the front door slam downstairs, voices yelling.

Magdelene relaxes. "It's okay," she says. "They're having a fight." I hear something crash downstairs. Magdelene gets the stuff back out of the drawer, holds a spoonful of it over the flame. "You don't mind if I do some, do you?" she asks.

I shake my head. I do not want to watch, but I cannot take my eyes away. I don't see how she can do that to herself, stick that needle in, but she does. She pauses while it's in there. "Sure you don't want some?" she says.

"No way," I say, and her eyes close while she pushes the rest in. She seems better at once when she takes the needle out. She's stopped shaking and she smiles at me. Downstairs her mother screams at her father. "Fuck you!" we hear her father say. Magdelene looks at me.

"Come touch me," she says, and I go over to her.

🐁

My mother finds my notebook while she's dusting my room. I don't find out till after everything's already happened, till she's already talked to my school principal, and to Miss Greenway, and to Magdelene's parents. I've gone for a walk; by the time I get back to the house, she's sitting in her seat at the dining room table, her eyes red with tears. I stop when I see her; my own eyes fill up immediately, my heart skips a beat inside me. I'm afraid that somebody else is dead, but then she gets up and walks across the kitchen and slaps me across the face. She's never hit me before. I just stand there, staring at her.

"How could you do this to me?" she screams, and then I see the notebooks, piled on the table.

"You went in my desk?" I say. I can't believe it. My mother never even talks to me. Why would she want to read the stuff I write? "What's the matter?" I say.

My mother stops, stares back at me. "What's the matter?" she says, aghast. "You're acting like a lesbian," she says, "your best friend's a junkie, your English teacher's condoning homosexuality and drug use, and you're writing lies about your family!"

"What are you talking about?" I say.

"You're not going to see her again," my mother says. "They've taken her away, and it's a good thing. That child needs an institution. And that teacher of yours..."

Something cold seizes my chest; it feels suddenly like my heart has stopped altogether. "What about her?" I say, and the words come out so slowly I can see them, printed carefully in midair.

"I don't know what she's been teaching you," my mother says, "but I'm going to make sure she doesn't do any more of it." She picks my notebooks up off the table like they're distasteful. "This is trash," she says, "pure and simple." She looks at me. "I'm ashamed of you," she says.

I grab my notebooks from her. I rip them out of her hands and I turn and I run out the door. She is yelling something after me, but the wind is in my ears and blocks it out, it flings her words back at her, hurls them in her face. I just run, keep running, clutching my notebooks to my chest and swearing I'll never stop, swearing they'll never, ever catch me, no matter how hard they try.

ten

May 1976

It is the end of my senior year in high school. I have a straight-A average, and a scholarship to a small college. I have made no friends during these past three years; I have spent them filling notebooks, and if now and then I have looked up from my books in study hall and let my gaze fall on the girls at the surrounding tables, talking about dates, tossing back their hair and clutching one another's arms when certain boys walk by, sending glances from the corners of their eyes that beckon and tease, if now and then I lay my pencil down and shake my head to clear it and watch their bodies move, I put the longing from me, file it away, and go back to my books.

I never saw Magdelene again. "Magdelene the whore," Frances called her. I think a lot of Frances these days, for want of a better target. I think of running into her again, and breaking all her teeth. They fired Miss Greenway. She came and found me before she left, found me weeping in the girls' room, my head buried in one of the sinks, hugging it as if it were Magdelene. "It's not your fault," she whispered to me. "Don't ever think it was your fault." She touched my hair before she left, for just a second, like a benediction, but I remember that she looked around before she did, and I remember, more than I remember the touch itself, how it felt when she took her hand away, as if the absence of it had been burned into my skin. She left me in the girls' room, holding the porcelain, pressing my face against it as if nothing else mattered.

My mother and I don't talk anymore. She tries sometimes, but I don't listen to her. I walk around her, look through her.

I'm just biding my time here, waiting till my sentence is up. I'm good at that. I've spent all this time studying, accumulating knowledge, and I've got a four-year scholarship to a liberal arts college. Only a couple of months to go and I'll be out of here. I'll have sprung myself.

●

Everyone these days is talking amnesty for the draft dodgers; in government class the teacher organizes debates, but they are listless ones. It is as if this is some piece of history. I sit and watch my classmates, fascinated. It is as if the war never touched them. They sigh and shrug and chew their gum, roll their eyes at one another when the teacher is not looking. I watch them sighing in their seats, stealing glances at the clock, and an anger grips me. It's the same anger I felt in childhood, sitting silent during the nuns' tirades. It's the same anger I feel for Frances, and for my mother, and for Magdelene's parents, for putting her away. I foster this anger, keep it fed and housed within me, give it water, and keep it alive. Someday I'll want it. When Judgment Day comes all I'll have to do is reach inside me and let that anger loose. That's all I'll have to do: open its cage and get out of the way.

In the meantime I pick up my pen and begin to write. I write about amnesty. I write about the war. I write about my brothers, about losing both of them. I write and I write and it does not occur to me that the bell has rung until the teacher is standing at my desk.

"What are you writing?" she asks me, and I hand it over to her. I don't even say anything, just give it to her and pick up my books and leave the room without looking back. It'll never matter again, who reads my stuff. Nothing will ever be private again.

●

When I walk out of the school building someone is waiting beneath a tree on the far edge of the parking lot. At first I do not recognize him, even as I head across the lot in his direction.

He stands there, with a cigarette between his lips and his jeans skin tight across his hips and his arms folded across his chest and his shaggy black hair hanging down past his shoulders. It's not until he turns his head and I see how long his lashes are that I realize it's Davey Janeski. He has grown up since I left that school. He is taller now, still rail thin but with some muscle now. As I get closer I can see that his eyes are still the same, deep and dark and shaded with the weight of those girl's eyelashes, and as I walk toward him he takes the cigarette from his mouth and throws it away and stands up straight, steps away from the tree so that I can see him full in the afternoon sunlight, and when I reach him he turns and begins to walk and I do not even have to ask him where we are going: we follow the same path down through town that we took the time before, except that now we are walking side by side, with the afternoon sun shining full in our eyes, walking until we reach the place where the path curves down into the woods and we leave the sunlight far behind, we leave it to the others in the town.

🖝

My government teacher asks me to rewrite my essay and to let her run it in the town newspaper. She tells me that what I have to say is too important to be left unsaid. She tells me this with her eyes straight on mine, but I don't give a damn. I shrug, and take it back, and write it over, and give it back to her. I don't care what she does with it. It's out of my hands now.

🖝

Davey Janeski asks me to my school's senior prom. He asks me in the parking lot, in the shade of the apple tree, after waiting for me again after school. All around us is the smell of springtime. High school is nearly over; it will all be over soon. There is a feeling in me that life will start after graduation, though I do not know what I expect. It seems to me that I have lived this part of my life so far waiting for my life to happen, waiting for it to take some form. My sentence is almost up.

Davey Janeski asks me to the prom and I don't feel anything. His eyes are black and huge and full of depths. His lashes brush his cheeks when he blinks. His is a baby's face, with a baby's rosebud mouth and tender nose, so incongruous with the tight jeans and thick black hair. It's a pretty face. But it isn't Magdelene's.

"Will you go with me, Maura?" Davey Janeski asks me, and it's the same voice I remember from the fifth grade, telling Chuckie Supulski to leave me alone. He's the same boy I kissed in the woods that day, when I wore his brother's sweatshirt and held his face to mine and let him desecrate a tree for me. He looks at me with his black eyes full of warmth, full of hope. He looks at me the same way Colin used to, long ago, when I told him stories and he held my hand and life meant more than it does now.

"Yes," I say, "I'll go," and Davey Janeski touches my cheek with his hand, for just an instant, and I still feel nothing. He turns and walks away, back through the parking lot, back toward his house. He is not Magdelene. He is not Colin. None of us is who we used to be. My heart stays still in my chest; it has been still now for a long, long time.

Colin wanders shoeless through the house; he makes no sound. He creeps from room to room, and he is always coming up behind us when we least expect him. He could be stalking us; he moves through the house like a wraith, sometimes standing unnoticed at our sides for whole moments before he chooses to indicate his presence. I watch him move his nearly fleshless runner's body with a lightness that is somehow not from grace, and I wonder if he has always been so quiet, so devoid of weight.

I stand in the kitchen, washing dishes. The window above the sink is open, the smell from the lilacs that line the house on its eastern side wafting in like perfume. I do this every night. It is my job. I do it well. My mother walks in while I am drying; I don't say anything to her. She stands there for a moment. I hear her sigh.

"You'll be leaving soon," she says.

I keep on drying, put each dish into the cupboard as I finish with it. I am leaving, and when I leave this house I will leave it for good. Life is out there, waiting for me.

I finish the dishes and hang the towel above the sink.

"Maura," my mother says, but I don't answer her, just switch off the light as I walk out, as if she isn't even there.

Davey picks me up for senior prom in his father's Pontiac, and I know when I see it that he has washed it for me. I greet him at the door in a long white dress with blue ribbon trim, a ludicrous dress, and when Davey pins my corsage to the front of it his face dips dangerously close to mine. I smell his cologne and it suddenly smells like Magdelene; it is so much like Magdelene that I nearly go limp and I suddenly want to seize his hands and hold them where they fumble, gracelessly, with the safety pins; I want to push his body back against the door and hold it there with mine, crush myself against him till the life is squeezed from that stupid, dying corsage and it drops to the floor and nothing is left between us but a few layers of useless clothing. I want to take his head in my hands and feel his mouth against mine, I want his hands to drop their flowers and undo the bodice of my dress. I want to pretend that he is Magdelene. I want to close my eyes and give myself over to this feeling, but my mother is standing there in the doorway, folding and unfolding her hands as if she were wringing the dishcloth between them, and Colin is creeping shoeless down some corridor, dodging us, and somewhere in the unlit kitchen my father is tossing down a drink, and snorting, and waving his hand, refusing to come out, refusing to see me off, and all I can do is hold myself still, clench my body until Davey

Janeski's hands have fallen of their own accord, and he holds the door open before me, with all the night sky open to take us in.

❧

"If only Colin would stand up straight," my mother says, unnecessarily, since I have no intention of answering her. She is chopping vegetables for dinner; I have come into the kitchen to get a glass of water. My mother sighs, as if she's been hurt somehow. "If only he'd put his shoulders back," she says, "and straighten up, but he's so bent over, all the time." She lines a row of carrots up, hacks their ends off. She is such a master at this cutting and dicing. She's so good at dismantling things.

I turn on the faucet next to her, fill my glass with water. As I do, I smell her powder, the faintest smell of roses, and that thing in me that I hold so tightly trembles for a moment, threatens to release. I take a deep breath and set my jaw. I will not let it go. I will not weaken. If I surrender I will die. Everything depends on just getting through this, on making it to that moment when I walk out that door and never come back.

My mother sighs again. "If only he'd straighten up," she says, "and look straight at you." I drain my glass and leave it in the sink, walk out of the room. She can chalk this up to bonding time.

❧

Davey Janeski holds his hands at the small of my back while we dance. I hold mine behind his neck. With an inch of space between us, we sway like stilted angels beneath the dim glow of the auditorium lights. The music seems to last for an eternity, and I want for it to end, for this senior prom to end, for the doors of the gym to open and for the lush black night to usher us back outside, to lift its finger and beckon us to it; I want to leave this place with its carefully gauzed lights and its chaperones, prowling the floor for transgressions.

🐦

"I don't know what to say anymore," my mother says. She stands in the doorway to my room, watching me work. "I don't know how to talk to Colin," she says.

I sit at my desk, taking notes from my physics manual, calculating distances and speeds. If I dropped my mother from a ten-story building, how long would it take her to hit the ground?

"Maura?" my mother says. "Do you hear me when I talk to you? I don't know how to talk to him." She pauses; I can hear the skip in her breathing, I can tell she's begun to cry. "I don't know how to talk to anyone anymore," she says.

🐦

Davey dips his head to mine. "Hey," he says, so softly I almost miss it, his breath a silent rush against my neck; "Hey, Maura," he says, and I lift my eyes to his. "Come on," he says. "Let's get out of here." He takes my hand, leads me off the dance floor, leads me out into the night.

The spring night air is full of the scent of flowers; I am full of the memory of Magdelene, sick with it. Lodged in my chest like a tumor, it weighs down my heart. I long for her. There are times I long for her so much I think that I cannot bear it anymore.

Davey reaches under his seat and pulls out a bottle of Jack Daniel's, passes it over to me. I put it to my lips and drink as if from a chalice, anoint my mouth with its contents as if with holy water. I pass it back to him and he takes a swallow, sets it on the seat between us. Then he reaches into the breast pocket of his tuxedo and pulls out a joint. "Do you smoke?" he says.

"Always," I say, and he hands it over to me. I put it in my mouth and light it, suck the smoke into my lungs until they can't hold any more, hold my breath until the burning in my throat is so fierce I have to open my mouth. I can feel my thoughts begin to break down, feel the ache in me start to lift. Maybe it doesn't matter; maybe it will be the same. Magdelene isn't here, but Davey is. Maybe I can make him do. I breathe in the pot and I hold it in my lungs and I think that anyone will do, just so I can get away from this prison that I live in, just for a while.

Davey pulls the car off the road at the first turnoff. Before he even gets the engine turned off I am on him, touching his hair, his face, his lips, his throat, his shoulders. He reaches for me and I close my eyes, touch my lips to his. We kiss and kiss and I try so hard, but he is not Magdelene, and for a moment I fear that no one will ever be Magdelene, but then his hands are unbuttoning my dress, and his fingers are on my breasts, squeezing my nipples, gliding down my stomach, and I open my legs to him, open them as far as I can, slamming my knee into the dashboard. I grab him with both hands and unzip his pants, pull him to me. I want his body, I want him in me, I do not want to remember Magdelene. I want to be free of her. I want to move on. I pull his body against me, feel the hardness of his dick against me, and I close my eyes and think that there is nothing that I will ever want more than Magdelene against me, than the softness of her body next to mine.

➵

"Oh, tell me," my mother whispers, standing in my doorway, "can't you tell me what to say to him?" I raise my eyes from my book, and look at her, standing there in the doorway, so small and thin and old. When did she grow so old? "What do I have to do," she says, "to make it up to you?" I look at her for a moment; her eyes are so dark in her face they seem to be burning holes there. "Can't we be a family?" she says, and I stand up at my desk and cross the room toward her, feeling her wanting me, and gently, so gently, I close the door between us, close it in her face.

➵

When Davey Janeski breaks into my body I feel torn aside, gained access to in a violence that makes me scream. I lock my legs behind his back, even as he thrusts into me, shudders into me as if he will never stop, while I feel the blood leaving my body in an endless flow and it is nothing like making love with Magdelene. It is nothing like making love. I lie there on my back with Davey Janeski coming into me and all I can think of is the front seat of the Pontiac, and how he will explain the stains to his father.

❧

When it is over, Davey sprawls on top of me, motionless, his eyes closed as if he were dead. I reach around him for the bottle of Jack Daniel's, which has ended up on the floor. I take a swig, spilling a little down my face in the process. I feel it soak through the bodice of my white prom dress, feel its wetness seep across my breasts, start to sink into my heart. Davey moans and starts to move; I wriggle out from under him. I pass him the bottle; he takes a drink. He starts the car with shaking fingers, puts it into gear, backs it out onto the road. We don't speak on the ride home.

We pull into my driveway and he does not walk me to the door. He stays in his car in the driveway, watching me walk to the door in my soggy, rumpled prom dress with the blue ribbon trim and bloodstains all along the back, and as I turn the key in the lock he backs up the Pontiac and drives back down the driveway, while I gather up my bloodstained skirts and slowly walk into the house.

❧

My father is waiting for me when I walk in; he holds a copy of the evening paper in his hands. It is three o'clock in the morning. I smell of whiskey and so does he. I am tired and dirty; my thighs are caked with blood. Somewhere Davey Janeski is off to scrub down Naugahyde. My father is standing in the hallway, blocking the stairs. There is no avoiding him.

"What the hell is this?" my father says, brandishing the newspaper in front of my face.

"It's a newspaper," I say. "Get off my case."

He opens it to the editorial page, to my article supporting amnesty. "What the hell did you write this for?" he asks me.

I shrug. "Couldn't think of anything else to do that day," I say. "It was just a whim."

My father stares at me. My mother appears from behind him and touches him on the arm, but he shakes her off. "Haven't we had enough trouble in this town?" my father says. "Couldn't you have let it go?"

I can feel that anger I have inside me, that body of anger that I have nourished and fed and caressed in me through the years. I can feel it stirring in there, lifting its head and looking around, shaking out its paws, sharpening its claws against the walls of my stomach. I can feel it begin to push against the bars. "Let it go?" I say to my father. "How the hell could I ever have let it go?" I look at him closer. "Who would ever let me let it go?" I say. "Not you. Sure as hell not you." Inside me, my anger circles the confines of its cage, whipping its tail. It is bigger than I'd ever expected. I don't know if I can keep a grip on it.

My father looks at me, his eyes narrowed, his breathing rapid. "You're just like him," he says, his voice so low I can hardly hear him. "You're just fucking like him." His words are slow; he is enunciating them around the alcohol, taking his time, carving space around him. "You look like him," my father says. "You act like him. You don't know how good you got it here."

"Where?" I say. "In this fucking country?"

"Shut up," my father says.

"Someday they'll give them amnesty," I tell him. "Nobody fucking cares about Vietnam anymore."

"I care," my father says. He crumples up the newspaper, throws it on the floor. "He'll never set foot in this house," my father says. "Not as long as I'm alive."

"You're right about that," I say. "Zach's too smart to come back here."

My father stops and looks at me. "Too smart?" he says. "You think he doesn't want to come back?" My father stares at me as if I must have lost my mind, and then he laughs, that hard and bitter laugh that has nothing to do with humor. "He's written a hundred letters to this house," my father says. "I don't read them — I throw them out." My father looks at me. "Because he's not my son anymore," he says. "Do you get it?"

Do I get it. I am standing in his hallway and something is beating in my chest like wings; any minute now that anger inside me will break out and obliterate everything in its path. "He's not your son anymore?" I say, slowly, and look my father in the face. "Who are you," I ask him, "the fucking Godfather? What right do you have to exile my brother?"

"You're just stupid," my father says, "all of you, stupid. Brainwashed."

"If anybody brainwashed me it was you," I tell him, "all these years I've lived with you," but he is already turning away from me, dismissing me with a wave of his hand.

"I could have brainwashed you," he says. "But I didn't."

"You did your best," I say, slowly. I am turning toward the door; even as I say it, something is turning me, placing my hand around the doorknob, and my mother is trying to get hold of my arm, saying softly, under her breath, "It hurts him, to see you turn against it all," but I am not listening to her; I turn once more, face my father's retreating back, and I say: "You took him from me. You took my brother from me. You drove him away and now you won't let him come back," and my father is facing me again, he is yelling, his voice cracking; "Get out," he is saying, "get the hell out of my house," but I am not listening anymore; I have my hand on the door and I am turning the knob and, taking my mother's hand from my arm, I am letting myself out the front door, walking down the steps to my car, and his voice is echoing after me, and that is the last I see of him, until now. Until his death.

eleven

When I go back to get my clothes, my father is gone. My mother hangs around in the doorway, one hand smoothing down her apron. "He'll get over it," she says. "You don't have to go." Her voice is soft as down in the air. It floats toward me, hangs about my nostrils, smelling of roses. It could smother me, if I let it.

I ignore her, just scoop my clothes up out of my drawers and throw them in my suitcases. I don't fold them, just hold them down with my knee while I pull the zipper up around them. It's like zipping up a body bag. I empty out my desk, my bookshelves. I take only what I need. I leave behind my childhood memories: my drawings, my stories, my stuffed animals. I keep it down to two suitcases and a book bag, things I can get downstairs in one trip. I don't look at my mother as I pass her. I hesitate outside of Colin's door for a moment. He doesn't come out. For a moment, my heart swells in my chest until I think that it will burst. Tears sting my eyes. For a moment, I think I cannot do it, and then I am walking down the stairs, toward the front door. My body moves as if on automatic pilot, carrying me toward my life.

I have to leave Adele with my parents. I know when I say good-bye to her that I won't be seeing her again. She's already eight years old. I see her eyes on me when I leave. They are as mute as Colin's. I look at her eyes and I harden myself. I gather myself up and let that anger in me turn to steel, fill me out. I will be strong, from here on out. I will not mourn my losses. I will never love anything again so much that it would hurt to let it go. That is what I tell myself. That is the oath I take.

❧

College goes like clockwork. Getting good grades is easy for me. I go to my classes and I take my notes and I go back to my room and I write my papers. I choose English as my major only because of Miss Greenway. I choose it for her, like an offering, at the end of my sophomore year. I don't stop to think what I'll do with a degree in it.

No one knows me here. I move about as if invisible. Weekends, I work at the local hospital, typing up OB-GYN reports. Nobody knows my name. I can move along these sun-dappled campus walks as thin and unnoticed as a shadow. I never speak in classes. I do not hang in crowds. I exist alone, invisible, waiting.

❧

Fall 1978

I meet Ilse in the registration line my junior year. She is standing just ahead of me, nearly six feet tall with light brown hair that floats down to her shoulders. When she turns and looks at me, I see that her eyes are a liquid brown and her skin is olive. I realize with a pang that her complexion is like Magdelene's.

"Crummy, isn't it?" Ilse says, indicating the line. She pulls a pack of cigarettes from her pocket and offers one to me. I shake my head. She puts one in her mouth and lights it with a match. The gesture is so familiar that it pains me; it inserts itself into my chest and pricks my heart like a needle. "Wouldn't you think they could figure out a better way?" she says.

I nod. I can't think of anything to say. I use my voice so seldom it's in danger of rusting. I don't talk even in class. This isn't hard to avoid, since most of the professors lecture, and none of them has ever told me to take a walk or to read aloud something that I've written.

Ilse studies me through her smoke. "What's your name?" she asks.

"Maura," I say.

"Maura," she says. Her voice is harsh, ragged from cigarettes. "I'm Ilse," she says.

"I'm glad to meet you," I say. I feel very small next to her. She is not only tall but broad shouldered, and she's wearing a brown leather jacket over tight black jeans. Her nose is slightly crooked, like she broke it in a fight. She looks me over, overtly; her eyes cruise my body. I feel movement in my chest, as if my heart were coming back to life, sluggishly, the ice around it beginning to shift and crack. It hurts, to feel it again.

"I am too," Ilse says, taking another drag on her cigarette. "I'm glad to meet you, too."

We stay in the registration line for an hour and a half. When we're done, Ilse asks me to come over for a drink. "We'll make some dinner," she says. When I hesitate, she pushes my shoulder, lightly, like a prizefighter. "Come on," she says. "You gotta live a little."

I struggle with myself a moment. My heart is fluttering within my chest like a small bird, learning to fly. It is perched on a branch, equivocating. Something shoves it off. "Okay," I say, not really knowing why. I head off across the campus with Ilse, into the setting sun, to do a little living.

🍂

Ilse lives with Renee in a dingy white house a few blocks from campus. The paint is peeling off, falling in flakes around the foundation. "Watch the bottom step," Ilse tells me as we head up the front stairs. The steps are caving in, rotted nearly through.

Ilse throws open the front door. The living room is large and dirty, cluttered with pillows and a mattress that obviously serves as a couch. "Honey," she says. "I'm home." Renee comes out from the kitchen, a slender woman with almond eyes and frothy black hair pulled back in a bandanna. She is wearing a peasant blouse that clearly shows the outline of her breasts and a long brown skirt and sandals. A huge tiger cat follows her into the room, rubs its head against her leg. Her legs are unshaven. She is beating something in a mixing bowl that she holds wedged against her hip.

"Hi," she says, and smiles. Her smile is languid; her features are soft, muted. "This is Maurice," she says, indicating the cat.

"This is Maura," Ilse says, going past her to the kitchen.

Renee looks at me, wistfully, a child's look. "How long have you been here?" she asks. Her voice is full of sympathy.

Her question startles me. "Where?" I say. "I just got here." I can feel my stomach tightening, a sentry starting its watch.

"No," Renee says. "I mean here on campus." She steps a little closer, still beating whatever it is she is mixing in her bowl. Her arms are thin and muscular; her skirt is flecked with paint. "I mean, we've never met you," she says.

"Do you want a glass of wine?" Ilse calls from the kitchen.

Renee takes another step toward me. Her eyes are huge beneath her bandanna. She looks like a refugee. Her smile is intoxicating. "I mean, you're really beautiful," she says.

I feel the blood rush to my head; for a moment I fear that I will faint. My heart is chugging like a freight train. I have spent so much time trying to keep it still. I cannot even breathe.

Ilse sweeps out of the kitchen to hand me a glass of wine, pausing to kiss the top of Renee's head. I wonder if they're lovers. "No," Ilse says, winking at me. "We're just friends." I wonder if I've said it out loud. I can feel myself flush.

Renee goes back into the kitchen, where I hear the clatter of pots and pans. I close my eyes, then open them. Ilse is sitting on the mattress, leaning back against the wall. She pats the seat next to her. "Come sit down," she says. She pulls an envelope from the pocket of her jeans. I marvel that anything can fit in there: they seem welded to her hips. She looks at me, her eyes sparkling. "Have you ever smoked a bong?" she asks.

"No," I say, clearing my throat. I feel like I've entered another world, like I've fallen down a rabbit hole and landed in an alternate universe.

Renee comes out with what looks like a kerosene lamp, sets it on the coffee table in front of us. "Oh, good," she says, clapping her hands. "I mean," she says, when I look at her, "it's so much fun when somebody doesn't know how to use it."

After dinner, we smoke again. Ilse hands me the lighter and I light the bong, slip my finger over the hole in the back, and inhale. The water bubbles up; the sound fills my ears. I breathe in deep and hold it, watch the smoke flood the globe of the bong, then exhale. I am such a quick study at this stuff. Beside me Renee lies stretched out on the mattress, one arm draped across the floor. "That's great," she murmurs, "great stuff." Her long hair, matted with curls, is barely contained by the bandanna. Her eyes are closed. She could be dead, the way she lies.

Ilse takes back the bong, relights it for herself, and inhales hard. It is getting late; outside, darkness is already beginning to fall. I lean my head back against the wall and let my brain mellow out. Ilse reaches across the mattress, takes my hand. We sit in silence together, watching the shadows on the wall. It occurs to me suddenly that maybe this is it, the thing that I've been waiting for.

I move in with Ilse and Renee a few weeks later. They make a room for me off the kitchen, a tiny blue room with a view of the trees. In it is one twin bed, covered with a blanket; one chest of drawers; one shelf of books; and a desk that faces the window. I move my things into it and it immediately becomes mine, my room, with its crumbling faded wallpaper covered over by posters, its blue rug worn nearly through in spots. Hundreds of people may have inhabited this room before me, just as they have this house, with its stained and leaning walls. It is an empty room; I sleep soundly in it. The people who have lived within these rooms are strangers to me.

There are no memories in this house that have anything to do with me.

🕭

When classes are over, I leave the English building and walk home through crisp leaves and air that is steadily growing cooler. This is such a quiet campus, quiet and still. There are no city streets to cross, no distracting traffic to dodge. I walk down gold brick paths that wind seductively between the red brick buildings. A gentle breeze moves my hair and touches my cheek. All around the campus lies a small midwestern town, surrounded in turn by cornfields. Along the side streets, the trees meet overhead. Everything is still. Overhead, the sky stretches a cloudless, placid blue, deepening now at the end of afternoon.

This small town is like the town where I grew up. I wonder why I couldn't have made it to a city somewhere. I wonder if this will be my curse, to live in a succession of small towns, with their continuous recycling of the same familiar street names. Water. Main. Elm. Walnut.

There is too much attention in a small town. Undivided attention and not enough people to divide it among. People invariably get more than their fair share.

I open the door to my house and Renee and Ilse sit at the kitchen table, smoking a bong. A bottle of wine sits open between them. Their hair shines in the light that comes in through the window behind their heads. Their faces as they raise them to greet me are rosy with wine, muted by pot. I stand in the open door and they smile at me, lazily, stretching themselves in the warmth of the afternoon sun at their backs. "Come on," Ilse says. "Come get stoned."

Darkness spreads through the house, passing from the streets and the trees and making its presence known along the floor. I inhale deeply and feel the lightness in my head expanding. So many evenings I spend stoned — first in the company of my housemates and then alone, in the darkness of my room. I sit cross-legged on my bed and feel bits of past and present intermixing throughout my mind while all around me the gold of twilight gives way to evening. Ilse and Renee move to the kitchen, put rice on to boil, dice vegetables. They don't care if I help or not. We all take our turns, here in our house. It is so far from the house where I grew up that I could be in a different galaxy. I write to Colin, now and then, but that is all. He never responds. Amnesty has come and gone, signed into law by President Carter amidst a flurry of public debate that burned itself out as quickly as a brushfire. Vietnam was a long, long time ago. No one really cares anymore. Amnesty has no impact on my life.

❧

Renee comes and gets me for dinner. I am sitting on my bed, writing in my notebook, when she slips into the room and curls up beside me on the blanket. Her fingers play in my hair, twisting it back and forth, stroking it. I feel like she is petting me, the way she pets Maurice.

"Do you want something to eat?" she asks me, settling her body alongside mine, resting her head against my shoulder. "It's good," she says, "tofu and stuff."

It is always tofu and stuff. Her body next to mine is soft and warm and gentle. She is boneless, like her cat. She can settle herself in anywhere. And she has claimed me, the way Maurice claimed her. She belongs to me.

I put my notebook down, lie back against my pillows, and put my arm around her. She sighs and snuggles in. Maurice comes in, looking for Renee. He sees me and frowns. He thinks I might be competition, and he's not entirely sure he trusts me. He jumps into my lap, turns around a couple of times, and settles in too, as close to Renee as he can get. Renee scratches his head, gets him under the chin where he likes it. They both close their eyes, Renee and Maurice, luxuriating in the cushion of my body. I think we must make quite a picture. We could be our own small family. We could be lovers, Renee and I, except that, for some reason, we're not.

❧

Tonight I am trying to study. I sit at the desk in my room and study history, rearrange my notecards and marvel at the way things fall into place. Ilse has a girlfriend over. I can hear them in the kitchen, moving around, laughing, murmuring, and more than anything else I can hear their silences: I can hear them standing in the kitchen in the darkness when they have ceased to laugh and ceased to talk and only move there, in the darkness behind that closed door, and in that silence my notecards and my books and all my journals seem purposeless.

I keep a bottle of whiskey beside my typewriter. I look at it now, uncap it and take a sip and feel it burn my throat. When I drink I feel the urge to write, to create. It's not a thing I can control; it's a passion, a desire, a drive to expel. It comes over me in that first light-headedness. It comes at night. It comes at times like this. It comes when I'm alone. It comes when there is nothing else to do.

❧

In the morning, Renee makes breakfast for us. She sets the plates on the table, dumps the eggs onto them. Ilse glances at me through bloodshot eyes; she is drinking tomato juice with vodka in it. From the bathroom, I hear the sound of the shower. Renee and Ilse exchange glances.

"Don't start," Ilse says.

"How was she?" Renee asks. She pours herself a cup of coffee and dilutes it with cream till it's almost white, sits down next to Ilse and stirs some sugar into her cup, then leans forward and waits, her face rhapsodic. She looks like she's the one who's just had sex.

"You're starting," Ilse says. She groans a little, holds her head. "I need some aspirin," she says.

I get myself some coffee, watch them. Ilse has a different woman every weekend. I wonder what she's looking for. Renee doesn't seem to have sex. She subsists on the details that she gets from Ilse.

Renee winks at me when I sit down, then reaches out and puts her hand on mine, holding it there, next to my cup of coffee. Maurice sits in her lap, kneading her with his paws. He glares at me. He still sees me as an interloper, though so far I am guiltless. "Good morning," Renee says to me.

"Good morning," I say, and sit and drink my coffee, feeling the warmth of her hand on mine.

twelve

March 1979

Renee is waiting for me on the porch swing when I get back from classes. She sits there with her head thrown back, her hair lifting gently in the breeze, one hand on Maurice, gently ruffling the fur around his neck as he lies beside her, trying to take up the rest of the seat so no one else can sit there. She is wearing a loose blouse that barely covers her breasts; her legs are tucked up beneath her. "Hi," she says, when she sees me. Maurice lifts his head a little, fixes me with an evil glare. Renee's shoulders are bare. Spring has not yet come here, and cold snaps in the air around us. I am wearing a sweater and a jacket; I can see my breath in the air.

"Aren't you cold?" I ask her. I myself am freezing. Renee sits there like it's summertime.

She smiles at me, that lopsided, wistful smile that transforms her face. "No," she says. And her hand when she takes mine is as warm as sunshine, as if she had her own personal heater somewhere. Her cheeks are flushed. She exudes heat; her skin is somehow tropical.

"I am," I say. "Let's go inside."

Renee shrugs and lets go of Maurice, who jumps down off the swing and stalks away, his tail in the air. "Okay," Renee says, and we go inside, Renee so close behind me I can nearly feel her breath on the back of my neck.

❧

Ilse isn't home from school yet. She has a night class on Tuesdays, then stays late to use the photography lab when no one else is there. I dump my books on the table by the door, unzip my jacket, and throw it on the couch.

"Do you want a glass of wine?" Renee calls from the kitchen. Before I can answer her she comes out with the bottle under her arm and two glasses in her hand. She sets them down on the coffee table, next to the bong. I sit down on the mattress, take off my hiking shoes, pull my sweater over my head. I am so tired of wearing winter clothes. I am so tired of waiting for spring to come. I feel like the snow that's been on the ground so long it's grown black and crusty, waiting for the thaw. Inside me, I am pacing, hungry for spring, lusting for the scent of green.

Renee fills the glasses nearly to the brim, hands one to me, then pulls a pack of matches from her pocket. Lighting the bong, she inhales, then pushes it to me. Her eyes shine in the half-dark of twilight, her skin golden in the shadows that stretch across the room. In this light, she could be Magdelene, handing me a cigarette, reaching over to light it for me, her face close to mine, the smell of her everywhere.

The pot hits my brain like a truck. I don't know how many brain cells it kills on contact. A lot, I hope. I hear the memory is the first to go. I hope so. I want to wipe my mind clean, start over. I want to sit here on this couch with Renee in the violet dusk of a dead but clinging winter and have no ghosts around me. I want to have no history; I want my life to begin at this moment, as if I had sprung fully formed into the world, twenty years old and ready for inscription.

I hand the bong back to Renee, sit back on the couch, and take a drink of wine. My hands are shaking. Renee takes them in hers, encloses them in her heat. "What's the matter?" she asks.

I close my eyes. In my private darkness, I see Magdelene, thirteen years old against a backdrop of still trees, her body lit by the sun that shines through their branches. Renee touches my face, strokes my hair back from my eyes. Her touch is tentative; her fingers on my hair are as light as a breeze. I open my eyes and she is right there, looking at me, though I can barely make her out in the darkness that is slowly swallowing the room. "Hey, it's okay," she says, and her fingers on my cheeks come away wet with my tears. I have not even known that I am crying. "Go ahead," she says. "Go wherever you need to," and then her arms are all around me, and my head is against her chest, and I can feel her breasts against my face, dark and heavy. I can smell her scent, vanilla and spice and something more, something dark and tropical, from deep in the rain forest of her being, and all I want is to lose myself in her, drown myself in her smell, let myself sink to the deepest, darkest place of her, the only place I can imagine being, the only place that I'll be safe, and her arms around me are strong as branches. Tiny muscles in her arms twitch against me, one hand strokes my hair back from my face, and her voice in the darkness is just a hush, a whisper on the breeze, a trace of water moving beneath the ice. "Just cry," she says. "Just keep on crying." And that is all I know, as the light drains from the room around us and Renee holds my body locked in hers and the darkness takes us in, sucks us deep into its womb and holds us there, rocking us gently through the night.

❧

Ilse wakes us when she comes in, somewhere around seven o'clock the next morning. She stops when she sees us, glances at her watch. "Aren't you guys gonna get up for class?" she asks. I try to sit up; the sun hits my eyes and I close them again. Renee tightens her arms around me, pulls me back against her.

"No," she says, pulling me to her and folding her arms around me. "We're taking the day off."

I try to look at her. "I can't," I say. "I've got a test today."

Renee holds me firmly. "Sshh," she says, kissing the top of my head. "I've got something to show you." I lie still in her arms. Her lips against my hair bless me, give me permission to surrender. I abdicate to her. There is nothing I can do.

Ilse shakes her head at us. "Suit yourself," she says, and heads for the kitchen.

"Where were you last night?" Renee calls after her.

In the kitchen we hear her banging around; I know she is looking for the coffee filters. Every morning she seems to forget where we keep them. I envy her her lack of memory. "Wouldn't you like to know," she calls back to us.

Wouldn't we. I lie on the mattress with Renee's arms around me and think that I couldn't care less; I think that the only thing that matters is where I have spent the night, that the only thing that will ever matter is how it feels to fall asleep and wake to the sound of someone else's breathing, to the feel of her heartbeat, next to mine.

❧

Renee hands me my sweater and my hiking boots, and brings me a cup of coffee, black and steaming, from the kitchen. "Don't shower," she says. I have no intention of showering. I want to savor the smell of her along my skin. She tugs a sweater on over her head, shakes out her curls, and reaches for her coat. "Come on," she says. "Bring your coffee."

We head out the front door and start walking. Renee leads me along a road that turns to dirt, narrows, and begins to rise. All around me are trees. "Where are we?" I ask her. "I've never been here before."

Renee, ahead of me, moves like a mountain climber. I never figured her for being in shape, yet I can hardly keep pace with her. "No one has," she says, glancing back at me over her shoulder. "No one but me." Her cheeks are flushed; her hair curls out beneath her cap. Her breath comes in and out in short, even gasps. We keep on walking, leave the town behind us like a discarded coat. The temperature seems to be rising as we climb; the sun above us illuminates our path. Renee takes a right off the road, into the woods. I follow her through the trees. The snow is deep up here, untouched by exhaust, white and unbroken except for the tracks of deer and some small animal. "It's just up here," Renee says. Her voice floats back to me on the breeze. I loosen my scarf, unzip my jacket a little.

"Here," Renee says, and kneels in the snow at the base of a tree. I kneel beside her; she parts the branches and leans in. "Look," she says, and I do. There, beneath the tree, tucked away from the snow, are the first faint shoots of spring. "It's coming," Renee says, looking at me. "Spring is almost here."

We kneel side by side beneath the trees. Above our heads a bird sings, hesitantly, as if she is just now finding her voice after a long, long time of silence. The woods cup us deep within their palms, breathe. on us to warm us. Renee reaches for my hand, squeezes it in hers. The sun beams on us. I almost think I see the green before us growing thicker, taking on weight, pulsing into bloom. "There," Renee says, softly. "You see?" I squeeze her hand back. We kneel there, in silence, listening to the bird's song, to the woods around us as they breathe, and sigh, and settle in around us, ready to take us through our lives.

Renee spends the rest of the day in her room, painting. I spend it lying on my bed, reading a novel. At the end of the day, she comes into my room. Her hair is pulled back from her face with a bandanna; her hands are stained with paint. "Come and see," she says, and pulls me to my feet.

The canvas is covered with oranges and pinks; it's an offering to spring, but a darkness lurks somewhere beneath the lines. There is no color for it. It is somehow inside the brightness, and it makes me shudder. I do not want to look too closely, for fear I'll make it out.

Renee touches my arm. Her eyes look tired now, lightless. "Let's go get something to eat," she says.

We head downstairs into the kitchen and make ourselves sandwiches with lettuce and cheese, some leftover chicken. We sit at the table and eat as if we have never eaten before. When I glance up from my sandwich, Renee is looking at me. My stomach drops a little, deep inside. Her eyes are the deepest hazel; they change from day to day, hour to hour. I never know if they will be green or brown or somewhere in between, flecked with amber. Chameleonlike, they adjust to the lighting of the room. Right now they are green, the color of moss clinging to a rock, deep in the woods, next to the creek. They are rich with the larvae of a million breeding things, damp with the air that lifts off the water. She could be a lizard, nearly indistinguishable from her surroundings, watching me from her sunlight, flicking out her tongue. I do not ever want to leave her. I want her to show me every breath of spring as it leaves her lips. I want to bury myself in her soil. I want her to give me life.

Renee pushes back her chair, stands up abruptly. "Come here," she says, extending her hand. "Come with me."

It is late in the day. We are entering that magic dusk. I take her hand and let her lead me through the doorway of the kitchen, toward the stairs, down the hallway to my room, where she folds back the blankets of my bed. We are alone in the house. The rooms are filled with our presence, suspended with our breath.

"Lie down with me," Renee says, and spreads herself on the bed, opens her arms. I slip into her embrace. "Take off your clothes," she says, but I can barely hear her words. She sits up, pulls her sweater over her head, pulls off her t-shirt. Her breasts hang, luminous, pendulous, incongruous with the thinness of her body. She slips her skirt off over her hips, lies brown and slender before me on the bed. She is so thin that I think I can see her heart beating beneath her breasts, moving the blood through her body. "Please," she says.

I stand up slowly, take off my clothes. My body feels awkward. I do not know if it is fat or thin. I feel no connection to it.

"You're so beautiful," Renee says. I wonder what she sees. How do I look to her, what does she see that I do not? "Touch me," she says, and I think of Magdelene lying in the woods, beneath the trees. "Touch me," Renee says, again, and I obey, touch my fingers to her face, stroke her cheek, trace the outline of her lips. She kisses my fingers, seizes my hand, and crushes it to her mouth. She runs her tongue along my knuckles, slips it deep between my fingers, takes my thumb into her mouth, sucks it so deep that I think that she will swallow it, draw my whole body after it into her mouth. The inside of her mouth is a vast cavern, its walls lined with velvet. Her mouth is a cave, closing in around me. She opens her mouth, lets me go, pulls me against her, presses her lips against mine. I open my mouth; her tongue slips between my teeth, serpentine, snakes through my mouth, brings it to life. I push against her as inside me something gathers, I run my hands along her shoulders, her arms, touch her nipples with my fingers, roll them beneath my palms. I kiss her mouth, her neck, her throat. I kiss her collarbone. I touch my lips to every part of her breasts, take her nipples in my mouth, feel them harden beneath my tongue. Something is alive in me; the ice is cracking, thawing; inside me something's shaking, taking me over. I run my hands down her stomach, slip my fingers between her legs. She moans, tips back her head; I run my tongue along her exposed jugular. Beneath my fingers a wetness seeps, a swamp; the room is full of her smell. She moves against my fingers, seizes my shoulders, presses her mouth to my breasts. I feel her tongue on my nipples. My breasts ache for her; she seems to swallow them into her mouth, and then my fingers have slid into the center of her, deep into her core, and she opens her mouth; her nails dig into my back. She screams, and her scream fills the room; she screams and screams and screams, and then her hands find my cunt and there is nothing I can do but move with her, and move with her, and my voice joins hers and there is nothing but the sound of us, and the smell of us, and the violent, utter depth of us, and we are lost to anything but the place where we are going, the place where we belong.

I wake to the sun in my face, and for a moment I do not know what has changed in the night. I am alone in the bed. I close my eyes and lie there, wonder if I've dreamt it, but all around me is the smell of her, the deep and musky scent of her body, clinging to my skin. I sit up and throw the blanket off me, slip my legs over the side of the bed, and stand up. My body catches me unawares in the mirror above the dresser. It is long and thin and fine; it is full of a grace and power that I never knew was there. My hair is wild, my cheeks are flushed. There is something animal about me, about the mound of hair that rises between my thighs, about the breasts that hide my lungs. I throw back my head and take a deep breath, feel my lungs expand, sense movement in the room. I close my eyes and let my breathing fill me, expand me, carry me up into the sunlight. The movement is my heart, brought back to life. My heart is beating, the ice has cracked; it thrives within my chest, a living, breathing organism, pumping blood throughout my being, giving fuel to my life.

I pull on my sweatpants, reach for my sweater, make my way into the hallway. My body feels weak somehow; my legs, unfamiliar. I feel as if I am just learning to walk, to put one foot before the other. The door to Renee's room is closed; she must be in there painting. I pause outside it, inhale again, try to revisit the smell of her that lurks around her doorway.

Ilse is in the kitchen, drinking a cup of coffee, when I walk in. I open the cupboard door and take out a mug, fill it with coffee, and sit down across from her. I feel shaky all over, as if I were recovering from the flu.

Ilse eyes me above her coffee cup. "Hmmm," she says, taking a sip. "I sense that something's happening here."

I take a mouthful of coffee; it's so hot it nearly scalds me, but I make myself swallow it anyway. It burns all the way to my stomach. I glance at her, trying for nonchalance. Her eyes are hard and beady and fixed on me. "What do you mean?" I say. I almost do not recognize my voice; it sounds almost girlish.

Ilse glares at me. "Don't give me any crap," she says. "There's been sex in this house and I know it."

We both hear the door to Renee's room open at the same time. She floats into the room wearing a kimono that sweeps the floor behind her. All her hair is hidden beneath her scarf. She looks like a wraith, like she's not even touching the earth. A smear of paint streaks her cheek. "Hi," she says, and her voice is deep with satisfaction. She slips behind me, wraps her arms around me, buries her chin in my hair. "Did Maura tell you that we fucked last night?"

I nearly choke on my coffee; Renee's arms are so tight around me I can barely breathe. Ilse only snorts. "I'm not like you, Renee," she says, opening up the newspaper to the comics. "I don't want to hear the details." We stay that way for just a moment, Ilse deep within her paper, Renee's head against mine, her breath against my hair. I wish that we could stay this way forever. To this day, I wish that we could have stayed that way. I wish that nothing had ever changed, in any aspect of our lives.

thirteen

Fall is everywhere in the air as I walk home from classes. It is in the leaves that lie scattered about the path beneath my feet, in the snap that I feel in my lungs when I inhale, in the promise that I feel in my brain. I am walking home to Renee. It is our six-month anniversary, and I am bringing flowers, a huge bouquet of irises and daffodils and baby's breath. All I have to do when I'm outside, walking like this, is breathe in deep and I'm right back in that barn stall, holding Adele in my lap and listening to her heartbeat, waiting for Colin to come home from school. The sun is shining, nearing twilight; rose-colored clouds weave themselves through the sky like garlands. Within me I feel a quiet peace. I am going home to my love. I walk as slowly as I can, savoring every step. I have begun to take my time, walking to and from the campus. There's no real reason to rush. Renee is always there when I get home. She is always there when I fall asleep at night, when I wake in the morning. I live in her scent, in the shadow of her gaze. I walk as slowly as I can, breathing and taking in my surroundings. I seem to have had so little time these past few years to see things.

I am filled with excitement, being involved with Renee. It gives my life another dimension. There's a lightness in my chest, a constant turmoil in my stomach. Every time I think of her, I feel something between exhilaration and nausea. If I catch a glimpse of her on campus, my stomach skips inside. I feel I can be anything I happen to be, even stupid, and it won't matter. My heart has been beating regularly these days, filling me with blood and life and expectation.

We are seniors now. After graduation, Renee and I have made plans to go to New York. We are going to pack up all our things — Renee's art supplies, my notebooks, all our books and clothes and pictures — and go live in the Village, starve in style. Renee's cousin has a lead on a place where we might stay. We have only nine short months to go, and then we'll be off, free of all of this.

I haven't gone back home since the day I packed and left. I haven't seen my father or anyone else. My mother writes me now and then, gives me news. Colin is still working at the bank, still doing the same job he has been doing for nearly eight years now. My father has had a few bouts of pneumonia, but he still won't give up cigarettes. My mother's garden is doing well, though she's going to cut down on the flowers next year; they're just a lot of work for no real returns. There is still no word of Zach. She wishes I'd come home sometime, pay them a visit.

They are such simple letters, written on rose-colored paper with lines that she adheres to closely, in handwriting that occasionally wavers. They make us seem a simple family, a typical family. They make the town that I grew up in seem so wholesome. The way she writes, it's like a Sunday school picturebook. I can see the life she describes all laid out like a drawing done in primary colors. It's a tempting vision; it lures me, much as the memory of Magdelene lures me. If I went back, I could try to track her down, see her. Would she recognize me? I dream sometimes of seeing her again, of catching her eye in a crowded bar or coffee shop somewhere, and having her wink. I dream of that moment of recognition, of the two of us together again, touching each other, dipping our fingers into each other as if into water, bringing up handfuls of each other to our mouths to drink.

When I think of Magdelene for too long, though, the picture goes dark. When I think of Magdelene, the colors fade and the storm clouds move in. I see the worms beneath the earth, eager to feed on what we leave behind.

I dip my head to the bouquet that I carry in my hands, inhale the scent from the irises. It smells like spring. It smells like the world did when Renee and I were first making love and everything was budding into life around us, filling the earth with color. Only a few more blocks, and I'll be home. Renee may have made supper; she may have gotten me some flowers, too. My heart catches for a moment in my chest, pauses for a beat or two, and then resumes. I never knew before what it is like to be in love. I never knew how wonderful it would feel, to live in the companionship of someone else. I had no idea what a blessing it would be.

The house is dark when I arrive. I carry the flowers up the stairs with me. Renee's door is shut, but a band of light shows beneath it. I hesitate outside the door. I want to knock, but she is probably painting. I do not want to bother her, but I can hardly stand having to wait to see her. I am about to go downstairs when Maurice appears in the hallway. He ignores me as he passes me, his tail lifted in disdain. Before I can stop him, he pushes the door open with his head, glancing at me for a moment as he crosses the threshold as if to tell me this is his privilege, not mine.

When the door swings open, I can see Renee inside, sitting on the floor, surrounded by canvases, her head in her arms, sobbing. I'm across the room in two steps; I lay the flowers on the floor and put my arms around her. "Renee," I say. "What's wrong?" Inside, my heart is beating so fast I think it will split apart, send my blood splashing everywhere, before I can find out what is wrong with her.

Renee doesn't look at me, just keeps sobbing into her hands. I keep one hand on her back, massage it lightly. Her body is so thin; these sobs seem much too large for her. I'm afraid they'll hurt her, the way they're tearing out of her. "Please tell me what's wrong," I beg her. "Please."

Renee takes a deep breath, looks up at me. Her eyes are swollen, rimmed with red. Her nose is running. She looks so beautiful when she cries. "I don't know," she says. "I don't know what's wrong." She squeezes out from beneath my arms and walks across the room, her arms clenched over her breasts, her back still hunched. She opens the drawer of her desk and pulls out a pack of cigarettes, shakes one loose and puts it in her mouth, tries with shaking fingers to light it. I take it from her hands, put it in my mouth and light it, then hand it back to her.

"I was just painting," she says, "and then I couldn't see the colors anymore; everything looked black, no matter what I did." She takes a draw on her cigarette, pulls the smoke deep into her lungs. She looks at me and shrugs, tries to smile, but her lips are trembling. She suddenly looks like a six-year-old.

I love her in that moment.

She laughs a little, unconvincingly. "I'm just being silly," she says, and walks quickly toward the door. "Come on, let's make some dinner."

"Renee," I say, starting to get to my feet, but she sees the flowers on the floor.

"What are these?" she says. "Are these for me?" She picks them up, cradles them in her arms. The bouquet could be a baby, the way she holds it.

"It's our anniversary," I say. "Six months." I feel stupid, suddenly. She didn't remember. I'm the one who's counting the days.

Renee stops and looks at me. Her eyes are dark, drained of color. Her face is streaked with tears. "Oh, Maura," she says. "They're beautiful." She comes back over to me, throws her arms around me. "Oh, thank you so much," she whispers. "Thank you so much for loving me."

I hold her in my arms, the two of us crushing the bouquet between our breasts. She is tiny in my arms, as fragile as the flowers that she clutches as if she'll never let them go. "I love you so much," she whispers, and I only hold her tighter. She loves me. She loves me. I hold her close, feel her body next to mine, smell her skin, mixed with the scent of the irises. Maurice glares at us from the bed, but I ignore him. I hold her and think that I'd do anything just to have her love me.

❧

It didn't happen only once, that I found her huddled in tears on the floor of her room. You would think I would have done something when she talked about the blackness in her paintings. But I didn't know what to do. I had my own blacknesses. It didn't occur to me that hers might have been different in any way.

❧

Ilse is ignoring me; she is taking nude pictures of Renee for one of her art projects. She spreads Renee out across the mattress in the living room, bends her arms and legs the way she wants them, snaps a series of pictures. I sit down and light a joint and watch them.

"Oh, wow," Renee says from the mattress, where Ilse has her on her knees, her back to the camera. "Can I have a toke?"

"In a minute," Ilse says, before I can respond. "We'll be done in a minute."

I sit with my back against the wall, smoke my joint, and watch them. They could be such a partnership, the two of them, Ilse with her long legs and her bomber jacket and her husky voice, Renee with her dreamy hazel eyes and earth mother breasts and flowing skirts. Renee looks beautiful, naked in this light. Her body is so small and spare, her face so wistful. She could be a child, kneeling there in the half-light that comes in through the windows. She is my lover, my partner. Of all the women she could have had, she chose me. I take another toke on the joint. I belong to her.

"Okay," Ilse says, snapping on the lens cap. "That's all for today." Renee stands up, shakes out her limbs, moves over to me, and wraps her body around mine, pressing her mouth to mine and drawing out the smoke that I have just inhaled.

"Oh, baby," she whispers, still holding the smoke in her mouth, her lips brushing mine. "Come upstairs," she says, and I let her take my hand, let her lead me up the stairs, let her make me feel beautiful again, full of the power of her love.

May 1980

The school year is nearly over. It won't be long before we graduate, before I have my B.A. in hand. Another segment of time is nearly up, another sentence served. I can feel that old familiar exhilaration budding in me like the leaves along the branches of the trees. I'm about to crest another hill. Surely my life will be out there now. Surely soon I'll turn a corner and there it will be, spread out in all its grandeur like an elaborate set, just waiting for me to enter it, stage left.

I walk as slowly as I can on my way home, breathe in as deeply as I am able. I have just about perfected the art of walking home, the zen of walking, from one place to another.

When I get to the house, Ilse is nowhere around. Renee is not on the porch, as she usually is, curled up at one end of the porch swing, her sketch pad in her lap, Maurice at her side, his head against her thigh, purring in his sleep. I skip up the stairs, open the door, drop my books on the table where we put the mail. No one seems to be home. The living room is empty, the mattress surrounded by glasses from Ilse's party the night before. A few empty gallon wine jugs litter the floor. No one's in the kitchen. The counters still bear the traces of our breakfast, splotches of spilled coffee, crumbs from our toast, some old tomato sauce that's been there so long we've gotten used to it. My room is empty except for Maurice, who glances at me sleepily, annoyed at the disturbance. Sometimes I'll find Renee asleep on my bed, her arms around my pillow, the corner of it in her mouth. I'll ease it out gently, put my lips in its place, and she'll waken slow and easy, stretching between my hands, rubbing the sleep out of her eyes, and shaking her head to clear it. "Oh, hi," she'll say, still limp with slumber. "I was just dreaming about you." She likes to sleep on my bed, she says, because it holds my smell.

But my bedroom is empty, and so is Ilse's, and so is Renee's. But the bathroom door is closed, and I can feel something in me start to click as I move toward it down the hall. It feels like a motor winding down, like my heart is shutting itself off, valve by valve. I put my hand on the doorknob, turn it, and push, and the first thing I see is Renee, sprawled on the floor, and blood on the walls, on the floor, on her, everywhere, it seems, but in her veins. Her body is so limp, so relaxed, that I know at once that it is empty of her. I know that she is not in the room: she has gone on, left me here; she's completing her life in some other place and time, and I'll never find her again; I'll never be able to live it with her. She's slipped out and rolled back the stone behind her so I can't follow her. She's left me here, bricked me back into my life, buried me alive in it, while somewhere she is out there, on her own, free of all of this.

fourteen

I still don't know why she did it. Even now, years later, I have no clue. I suspect she did it on a whim. I suspect she had no reason, that she was standing in the bathroom, washing her face, brushing her teeth, combing out her hair, looking through the medicine cabinet for the deodorant, and that the idea came to her and she suddenly couldn't think of any reason not to. Standing there in the sunlight coming through the window by the sink, illuminating her perfect body — it probably just seemed like the thing to do, at the time. If any one thing had been different, it might have changed everything. If it had been raining, or if she'd had a class to go to, or if I'd stayed home from school...

But I could go mad, thinking of this. If I think of her too long that quicksand will suck me into it. If I don't get a grip on solid ground, that muck will envelop me, fill my nostrils, close over my head, hug itself around me till I die.

I cannot think about it.

Surviving her is endless, like trying to free myself from the grasp of a crippling illness by sheer force of will. At first I don't think I'll be able to keep going. Something brings me back, again and again, to the sink in the bathroom, to my face in the mirror. I think she must have left a crack somewhere, a place for me to get through, but my fingernails scratching the glass catch on nothing. There is no way out. I am locked into my life. I stumble through it, mechanized, doing my duties by rote, drinking my coffee and dressing my body and clicking myself on for the day and off for the night. I move through the days like clockwork, until finally I begin to dream of her whole, as she was, unscarred, floating through my sleep like a vision, kissing shut my eyes, lulling me to rest.

To this day, I wonder what my life would have been like if I'd gotten involved with Ilse instead of Renee. We probably would have had a couple weekends of passionate sex, then looked at each other one morning and thought simultaneously: Nah. We probably would have shaken hands and called it a day.

Or maybe it would have worked. Maybe we would have looked at each other over our coffee cups and just as simultaneously fallen in love. We could have moved to San Francisco after graduation, gotten motorcycles and ridden them west into the sunset, gunned our engines across the desert, wearing our leather jackets and our skin-tight jeans and our boots, leaving all our baggage behind, neatly shelved away in the closets of our decrepit house, ready to be inherited by the next set of renters.

But I didn't get involved with Ilse, and she left after Renee's death and headed west by herself. She couldn't stay around there anymore, she said. She got her diploma and took off alone. The last I heard of her, she'd taken up hang gliding somewhere outside of Taos. I can still picture her, soaring off over the Rio Grande, her arms outstretched and her feet dangling, winged like a hawk, gliding on the air, a kind of Amelia Earhart, pursuing her own trip. I didn't get involved with Ilse. I got involved with Renee. I have to survive her.

And so I get my diploma and I go on to graduate school, and when I get out, I take this job out here, bury myself in these mountains where I know no one will ever come. I avoid having lovers. I avoid having friends. Deep inside, on an honest day, I would say that I fear there is something about me that causes people to leave. I don't know what it is. Maybe something planted deep inside, activated by the beating of my heart, sends out a signal to people, so that they take one look at me and know they've got to get out fast.

I could take it as a compliment, that I inspire such extremes.

But more often it feels like a curse. I feel like I have a brand on my forehead that keeps people from me. Or perhaps it keeps me from them.

I don't know the answers. I live here in my two-room apartment above the antique store and when five o'clock comes the lights in the store go off and I'm up here all alone, except for Earl, and his wife, and his dog. And Maurice, who has claimed me for his own, in the same way that his previous owner did, so many years ago.

I write a lot of letters to them, these people who have left me. I write to Magdelene. I write to Zach. I write to Renee. I tell them where I am and what I'm doing. Sometimes I tell them what I'm thinking. There are times, when I'm sitting at my desk with my fingers on the computer keys, that I want to tell them everything, everything I feel. I try to block the urge out: I shut off the computer and go hold Maurice, or gather some recyclables for Earl, or grade some compositions. But sometimes I sit back down and turn on my computer or open up my notebook and then I tell them everything — about the doubts I have about my teaching, how I fear I'll turn into Sister Martha, start playing on my students' vulnerability, exacting their contrition and using their confidences, holding them up for ridicule. I tell them how I want to love again, how I wake at night and want someone in my bed with me, someone's body next to mine. I tell them how I walk at night, down to the fountain in the center of town, and how when no one's looking I throw a quarter in it, now and then. Not even a penny; it's gone that far. I tell them about my loneliness. I tell them about the ache in my chest where my heart used to be, before I reached into myself and tore it out by the roots and flung it from me as far as I could. I tell them how my lungs have healed over it, how my skin has closed again, left a scar that runs the length of my body, from my throat to my breasts to my cunt, how hard it is to breathe, with all that emptiness in there.

I no longer write to Colin.

❧

Sometimes my evening students take me out after class; they settle me down at a corner table in the local bar and place a pitcher of beer before me. "So what are you doing here?" one asks me. "How on earth did you get here?"

"They offered me a job," I say, sipping my beer.

"How old are you?" Tony asks me. Tony is an Italian-descended student from Philadelphia, majoring in computer science. It hardly fits the greased-back hair, his deep black eyes, the south Philly accent.

"Shut up," Matthew says, nudging him. "Don't ever ask a woman her age."

"So what's the deal with you?" asks Tony. "Do you got a boyfriend? Are you gonna get married?"

"Geez, leave her alone, man," Steve says, but as I glance around the bar I suddenly find myself looking at Liz, the short-haired student from another class, sitting with her girlfriends in another corner of the bar, looking at me with her breathless, gray-green eyes.

"Ask her something else," Matthew says, and across the bar Liz looks at me as if still waiting for my answer.

❧

There are moments, in the evening, when I am suddenly aware of the loneliness, as tangible as a body beside me on the couch, when I can find nothing — no book, no thought, no walk or movie — to fend it off, to put it from me. There are moments when my solitude reaches for me and draws me to it in an embrace too close for comfort. There is nothing I can do but wait for the moment to pass. There is nothing I can do but clench my teeth and close my eyes and wait for the loneliness to go away. There is no other option.

❧

I have made my choices, and I live my life. It is not the life that I thought I would live. It is not the life that I pictured for myself, that mirage glimmering on the horizon up ahead, drawing me on, feeding on my thirst. I have come to think that life is just a thing we do, a series of steps. It doesn't really matter where they go. Only the walking of them matters. Only the movement counts. There will never be any more than that.

I live in my apartment, alone with Maurice. I go to work, I do my job; I do it well. I write in my notebooks, I read my novels. I take care of Maurice, hold him to my heart. I try not to imagine what life could have been.

I seldom think of Colin these days. I know from my mother's letters that he's married now, and has two sons: Reuben is studying the violin, Will has a home computer. I know that his wife, Ruth, teaches part-time at a nursery school and that Colin has formed a running club and runs races throughout the state. I know that Colin is still at the same job in the same bank. I try not to think of Colin, stuck back there, mired in old mud, spinning his wheels. Instead, I center my thoughts on Zach, the one who freed himself. I imagine him at twenty-two, leaving his country; I imagine him crossing the border. I imagine a lot of things as I sit alone in my apartment night after night with Maurice. I imagine a lot of things about Zach's life, to keep from thinking about my own.

The college where I teach is a tiny one, in a small mining town in the middle of nowhere, blocked out from the rest of the world by a range of mountains that come all the way from the Appalachians. We are equidistant from five major population spots: Toronto, New York, Philadelphia, Pittsburgh, Cleveland. In five hours, you can be somewhere. Meanwhile, you are here, in a quiet mountain town, recycling memories and dreams, because nothing new will ever happen to you here.

All my colleagues are some twenty years older than I am, which means, I realize belatedly, during one of our department meetings, that they came here during Vietnam. This means they were the age that I am now, and teaching college, during the unrest, the protests and the demonstrations. I watch them dubiously throughout the meeting, trying to picture them with sideburns and bell-bottoms, flashing the peace sign and smoking grass with their students, but I can't. I cannot imagine them in an earlier time. I cannot imagine them any way but the way they are now: aging, set in their ways, devoted to their lectures and their bibliographies and somehow Victorian in their orientation. I cannot imagine any of them in the act of making love, in any time period.

My students have no memory of Vietnam. They are only about ten years younger than I am, but they have no remembrance of it. When they grew up, we were out of Vietnam. It is as if I fell between generations — mine has vanished somewhere and I do not know where it has gone. The people who were active in the sixties have settled down now, made their peace with 'Nam. These kids now know it only as history: they study it, regard it politely as a kind of relic, an eccentric blip in the course of a century. But for those of us who were children in the sixties, too young for our own activism, too old for innocence — for us there is no place anymore. We had no place to start from. We existed in the crack between two generations. I look at my students now and I wonder what's important to them. Who are they, really, and what will happen to them?

❧

I am the only person my age I can find in this area. The students are all under twenty-two; everyone else is at least past fifty. Everybody tells me this is a favorite area for retirees from the City. I'm never sure which city they're referring to, but certainly people can buy a house here for next to nothing and pretend from the gaslights that they are in New England.

I rent my apartment and I live my life. I live it with determination. I have my furniture and my lace curtains, my prints on the walls. They are Georgia O'Keeffe prints, huge wide-open flowers that remind me of Renee. I try to settle in. I spend my mornings teaching, my afternoons preparing lesson plans, and if when evening comes I wish that I had left behind some clues, some trail of bread crumbs, to lead somebody to me, I will not admit it to myself, and so the time ticks on endlessly, solidifying into the past.

�◗

I take Maurice to the vet for his shots, and to my surprise there's a new vet, a woman, young, with reddish hair and a trace of freckles. She wears blue jeans and running shoes, has her hair tied back from her face. She smiles at me.

"Where's Fred?" I say.

"He's not treating small animals anymore," she says. She turns her attention to Maurice, lifting him out of his cat box with surprising deftness. "So," she says, "where do you come here from?" She knows immediately, I note, that wherever I am from, it is not here.

I tell her as I watch her pet Maurice's head, catch the fur at the back of his neck and tip it back, pry his mouth open with fingers that clearly do not mess around.

"How long have you been here?" she asks me. Her fingers probe and prod Maurice, turning him and rearranging him on the table like so much molding clay. She has long fingers, piano hands. They are strong and broad, heavy knuckled. These are hands she uses in her life.

I shrug. "A couple of years," I tell her.

She glances up at me. "Ah," she says, "you're still a newcomer."

I wonder how long I'll have to live here before people stop saying that. I sense I'll never live here long enough. "Why?" I say. "How long have you been here?"

The vet gives Maurice his shots, slips him back into his box, and snaps the door shut. I can feel his relief. "All my life," she says, tallying up the costs on her invoice form, "except for school." She sweeps her hair back from her face. I can see the wrinkles around her eyes when she frowns, lines of concentra-

tion. I notice that she wears no wedding ring, and curse myself
for noticing.

�·

I take a long walk every night before bedtime: along Main Street
and then up toward Walnut, past the big houses occupied by
tiny senior citizens who have moved here from the city seeking
a cheap place to die. I pass cemetery after cemetery — there
seems to be one on every street. I walk and walk and walk, and
the sky seems more distant than it ever has before. It is so dark
up here in this corner of the country; I have never seen a place
so dark. I take my solitary walks and tell myself that this is what
I want: a healing time, for introspection.

It is quiet when I walk at night. I walk down side streets,
past houses, staring into windows as I pass. I see girls playing
pianos, hair bound behind their heads; I see boys playing catch
in driveways; I see women serving dinners, men drinking beer.
I see America in these windows, and I see it from my sidewalk,
walking with my hands in my pockets, stealing my vision of it
from them, a thief.

It could be the same small town where I grew up. These
could be the same small families, living out the same small lies.
One of those little girls could be shooting up in her bedroom
upstairs, surrounded by her dolls. One of those little boys could
be forming a pack with his friends, hunting for prey. One of
those women could be spying on a neighbor, looking for
information to hold over her head. One of those men could be
a preacher, writing sermons on the outcasts in the town.
Somewhere in this town there are other kinds of families —
women living with women, men with men, single parents,
blended families — but I do not see them through these
windows; they must take care to keep their blinds closed. Only
the approved advertise themselves. I walk in my darkness,
alone on my sidewalk, letting the chill of the air penetrate my
lungs.

●

Somewhere a car slows, skids on ice, rounds a corner, and draws up to a curb. Its lights shut off. The passenger door opens slowly. There is no light to illuminate the figure ducking around to the driver's side, but I know right away that it is Zach, shaking the hand that extends from the driver's opened window with a quick, firm movement that takes less than a second before the window has been rolled up again and the car thrown into gear. The tires slip as the car begins to move away; there is a moment of spinning, and then the tires catch and the car rolls free, sliding off around the corner onto a path invisible to Zach, who is left standing by the side of the road, against a backdrop of abandoned warehouses and shattered streetlights, holding a duffel bag in one hand. For a moment he just stands, as if to let his eyes adjust to the lack of light, and then he turns and is swallowed up by the darkness that shrouds the empty street like the lid of a coffin, closing.

●

In class somebody mentions values. "What do you mean?" I ask. "What's a value?"

Liz meets my eyes. "Family?" she says. There's a question in her voice, like she thinks this might be an answer I want.

"Is that a value?" I say. Or an institution? I want to add, but I feel that I am treading on thin ice here. Earlier in the semester, when I asked these students what they believed in, Patty raised her hand and said: "Jesus Christ, our Lord and Savior." That killed the discussion.

"I don't know," Liz says.

"What do you value?" I ask her. There's a moment of silence. I wonder if I've gone too far, crossed that line that separates the classroom from the personal.

Liz is looking at me. Her hazel eyes are full of light from the sun coming in through the classroom window. "I value love," she says. "I value commitment. I value monogamy." Her eyes on mine are steady; they issue me a challenge. "What about you, Maura?" she says. "What do you value?"

I can feel that sluggish skip of my heart within my chest, compressed beneath my breastbone, where I prefer it to slumber, enabling me to pretend it is not there. What do I value? "Independence," I say. "Precision. Fighting back."

They are all looking at me now. I wonder what I'm talking about. Are these the things I value? What about love and commitment? What about honesty? I think. What about justice? Honor, I start to say, but the class period is up; already Patty is gathering her things, Matt is looking at his watch. Wait, I want to say, let me start again. But the chimes are sounding the hour, and they are all heading for the door. Liz is stuffing her books in her bag. Wait, I want to say. I wasn't telling you the truth. Liz's cheeks are flushed; she thinks that she said something stupid, talking about monogamy. Give me another chance, I want to say, but she has swung her bag over her shoulder and left the room, not looking at me. I am left at my desk, alone in the circle of desks. Why do they seem so far ahead of me at times? I wonder. How did they get such a jump on me, how did they come to think so clearly, to know so absolutely?

❧

Maurice develops a cough and I have to take him back to the vet, who takes his temperature and feels his glands and bends down to look into his eyes. Maurice spits at her and I feel somehow responsible, as if he may have hurt her feelings. "Here are some antibiotics," she says. "Bring him back in ten days if he isn't better." She hands me the packet of pills and the cat box, containing Maurice, sending me home with a smile that seems to flood me to the roots. I go back home and hold Maurice on my lap and think about slipping my hands into the pockets of those blue jeans, undoing the clasp that holds that hair back, touching those freckles with my tongue. Maurice huddles in my lap, secure of my love in his misery. I hold him a little closer, feeling somehow responsible, as if my neglect has brought him to this, and I'll never be able to repair the damage.

❧

Somewhere there are footsteps, muffled, almost silent, the footsteps of a man in heavy boots moving quietly through snow. He moves with purpose through the falling snow of a predawn winter darkness, somewhere so far north that it seems the sun will never rise. He squares his shoulders and I see that it is Zach, ducking for cover between two buildings. A winter wind that is colder than anything he has been used to slips through the knit of his scarf like the blade of a knife. In one hand he grips his bag; in the other, a slip of paper. He turns off on a side street and walks with his head up despite the wind, searching the doors on either side for numbers that will tell him something.

❧

I wonder if Zach remembers me at all; I wonder if he ever thinks about me. It hardly seems fair, that I could not exist for him. But if I do, then why has he never written to me? Why have I never seen him? Were we so easy to get free of?

I sit at my window grading papers, looking out over the small town that has become a kind of home. Outside, it is raining; I sit at my desk with the lights turned off and work by the light that comes in off the street, the main street of this town nestled among these mountains. I sit at my desk in the near darkness, hidden by lace curtains, watching the rain fall to the street. This is my town now, and I watch it from my second-story rooms, silent in the night.

❧

Liz comes by my office before class. She's cutting into my preparation time, but I don't care. Just the sight of her brings a lump to my throat. She sits down on the edge of the chair beside my desk, as far away as she can get. "Was it stupid, what I said yesterday?" she asks.

I put my pen down, turn to face her, feeling tired beyond my years. "No," I say. "Those are real values. What I said was stupid."

"Was it true?" Liz asks me, both hands tight on the book bag in her lap. My throat aches, watching her. She has such dark skin, such defenseless eyes.

"I don't know," I say. "I don't know what I believe in."

Zach finds the right house, knocks twice, as prearranged, then twice again. The door opens, just a crack, just enough to let him in before it shuts again, shuts out the wind and the cold and the deep and northern darkness that prowls all up and down the street.

"Do you want to get a cup of coffee after class?" Liz asks me. She sits like she's about to run, every muscle tensed and ready. Her hands grip her bag so tightly, it might be a sword or a shield.

"I can't," I say. It's hard to get the words out. They feel stuck somewhere in my throat.

"Why not?" Liz says. A hint of fire sparks deep within her eyes.

I make myself look at her. The scar along my breastbone seems to open like a furrow, exposing me to her. "You're my student," I say. I look back down at the papers on my desk, lit by the light from my lamp. "I just can't," I say.

There are two of them, a man and a woman. They own a motel; they take Zachary and put him in the single way at the end, to let him rest. Their son shows him to it, unlocks the door with the key, and shows him how to lock it from the inside. Their son is nearly the same age Zach is, and the two of them stand there for a while, in the room, talking. The son has been border running for some time now; he is ingenious at it, hides the guys'

papers in his hubcaps. While they are talking, a knock comes at the door and my brother opens it to a young woman, the same age they are; she's the daughter of the couple, sister of the man in the room with him now. She has a flask of rye in her pocket, offers him a slug. She has long, dark blonde hair that parts across her forehead and falls into her face. She has deep blue eyes. She is the first woman that my brother loves, and she will not be with him for long.

"But I saw you having beer with your other students," Liz says.

"That was different," I say. I feel old again, ready to be laid to rest.

"I'm not a kid," Liz says.

I look back at her. Her skin is golden in the light from my lamp. There is a great weight within my chest, as if my heart has turned to stone. No. She is not a kid. "It doesn't matter," I say. "It's not about that, really."

The motel owner's son comes for him the following morning, takes him with him on his roofing job. Zach learns the trade, learns how to handle a hammer, how to line up shingles, how to true a piece of wood. He works all day long in the cold; at the end of the day he has a drink with the motel owner's son. He can feel his muscles, sitting there at the bar with a beer in his hand. He can feel his body, hard and foreign, and he is proud of it.

"What is it about?" Liz asks me. "Is it because I'm gay?" she says. "Are you afraid that people will start talking about us?"

"No," I say. "That's not it at all." Her eyes hold mine, and I see that she is trying to see behind them. She is trying to find me. How can I tell her that I really just don't know? That it's myself that I'm afraid of. It's me that brings me fear.

🐦

Zach finishes his drink and throws his arm around the shoulder of the motel owner's son. Together they head for the door. He is happy, expansive. He has a job and a place to live, a place to come back to. He has a whole new identity. He is starting over again, twenty-two years old and smarter now, with all the benefits of youth.

🐦

Colin holds my hand and leads me through the woods as if he were my father, my caretaker. The day is crisp; it is fall, and all around us the trees sparkle in a sun that filters through their leaves and dapples the ground. The air stings our cheeks. It is a midwestern fall day and Colin's fingers are closed on mine and he never walks too fast for me, despite his height. His eyes are dark; a light wind lifts his hair. He looks like a boy, red-cheeked on an autumn afternoon, like there is nothing on his mind but a walk in the woods in a crisp space of time holding his little sister by the hand. You have to look close to see the shadows in his eyes.

🐦

I cannot concentrate tonight. I can't grade papers when all I can see is Liz's face, tight and earnest, in my office. It's late now; I think that I should go to bed, but before I know it I am putting on my sweatshirt, zipping up my windbreaker, letting myself out of the apartment, and slipping down to the street. I step outside and begin to walk, my hands deep in the pockets of my jeans. A full moon precedes me as I walk. Hanging up there, it looks like it's moving and I'm standing still. A group of clouds is heading toward it on the run, like they're hunting it down; they reach for it headlong and it shines right through them. It just floats there and lets them come for it like it knows: they sweep right up on it and it beams right on through like a headlight, like a beacon; it moves steady on through the sky and leaves those clouds behind and all around it the night sky hovers heavy with snow and cold and a wind whips up and rattles the lampposts and pushes my hair from my ears and that moon just hangs there, silent, moving toward me almost imperceptibly, like the hands of a clock, except that I'm the one that's moving, and all around me the streets are silent, and it's time to go back home, time to go to bed, and tonight, as every night, I want to keep on walking until I've covered every street there is. I want to keep going, and feel the pavement move beneath me. I want to walk until I've nothing left, till I've spent all the strength that's in me. I want to feel it leave me, this energy, the relentless urgent energy that besets me every night and will not let me sleep or rest. I walk and walk and nothing quiets this rampage in me, nothing eases it, and I just keep walking, dropping my shoulders and gazing up at the sky and breathing in a slow, even rhythm.

I walk through the village green. I walk through this green every night. Built in 1835, it lies across from the courthouse in a mist of nonchalance, a square of ground surrounding a fountain at the center of town.

The fountain consists of fairy-tale figures, Winken, Blinken, and Nod, suspended in a wooden shoe, the bronze of them gone green with age. All around them on the green stand proud memorials of war — testaments to soldiers and sailors, World War I and World War II, Korea, Daughters of the American Revolution. There is no mention of Vietnam. You would think that that war had never touched this town, except that I have found, hidden in its graveyards, the graves of those who died there.

Just up the street is an old white frame church. The Masons meet there every Wednesday at 6:45. I've always liked to go up there at night and sit, silent, on its steps. I didn't find the churchyard that surrounds it, with all its graves dating back to the 1840s, until one afternoon, in daylight. Such an old town, this is, an old town that stopped some time ago. All that time I'd been sitting in the middle of a cemetery and never knew it, sitting with my hands clasped, gathering strength for the walk back home.

I wonder what I'm doing here, living alone in this small town. I wonder why I live alone, what I'm scared of, in this life.

🔊

Back at his room, Zach shakes the hand of the motel owner's son, claps him on the shoulder, and sees him off. He turns and unlocks his door then, and pushes it open and steps inside, warm, happy, full of beer and conversation in the frigid cold that is his home. He shuts the door behind him, doesn't lock it. Turning toward his mirror, he unfastens his shirt.

🔊

I go back to my apartment, pull open the door, pet Maurice, make myself some coffee, and sit beside my windows with their flowing lace curtains filtering the sounds from the sidewalks below. During the day, the sounds are of people walking, pushing baby carriages, talking, fighting, calling absently to straying children, greeting neighbors on the sidewalk opposite. Now and then on a Friday night, there are sounds from the bar across the street, which, at closing, spills its patrons out into the street beneath my windows, where they argue, push one another, sometimes fight; one night I woke to screaming — the man: *Go on, go home to your kid* — the woman: *You're never there, you're never ever there!* There is so much life on Main Street, so much feeling, and I sit behind my curtains, invisible within my walls, and feel its stir.

🔊

The motel owner's daughter drops by Zach's room that night, pushes open the unlocked door, and offers him a shot of rye. He turns to her when she enters, takes hold of her hair, pulls it back from her face, touches her cheeks with his fingers, takes the flask from her, and puts it on the table. She is long-legged and spare; she can wrestle him to the bed before he has time to get his breath. They lie together on the mattress, breathing hard, laughing at their eagerness. There is nothing to get in their way, no one to come between them. No questions are asked, no answers given. He pulls her down on top of him, pulls her face to his, and they make slow, poetic love in the flashing neon light of the motel sign.

🖤

On the street below, a door slams. Somebody shouts, feet slap the ground running. You could almost think, sitting up here in the dark, above this Main Street antique store, that you were in a city, for all this noise.

🖤

Before long Zach is organizing border runs for the family. He cannot do the runs himself — that would be too risky — but he can send the daughter on some of them, and she complies without complaint, pocketing her rye and kissing him farewell, always as if each time were the last.

🖤

Shortly after Thanksgiving, I take Maurice back to the vet. She smiles at me when I drag Maurice's box into her examination room, turns to the counter behind her to dig out his card.

"How was your holiday?" she asks, her back to me as she flips through her index cards, looking for my name.

"Fine," I say. I do not want to tell her that I spent it grading research papers; this seems too pathetic even for me. I want only to stand here, one hand on Maurice's head, the other on his body, and look at the flow of her back into her hips as she stands there, the way her blue jeans hug her ass. "How was yours?" I ask.

"It was quieter than usual," she says. "Our daughter came home from college." She turns back to face me, Maurice's card in her hand, her hair falling forward like rain. "My husband's parents were out of town," she says, pressing her fingers along Maurice's body, "so it was just the three of us."

I am looking down at Maurice; a moment passes before I can raise my eyes to look at the vet. She has a husband. She has a daughter in college. I glance down at her hand. She is wearing a wedding ring. I wonder if I'll wake up from this someday and find that life is more than a series of cruel jokes. She fills her syringe, gives Maurice his shot.

"There," she says, smiling at me. There are lines all through her face. This is a woman who lives her life, who lets it carve its path in her, stroke by stroke, to remember it by. I close Maurice back up in the cat carrier and put him in the car. The vet doesn't charge me for the office visit.

When I get home, I sit down at my window with all the lights turned off. I don't know what is happening to me. I feel suddenly pathetic, for being thirty years old and still alone for the holidays, for not having made a family for myself, for not at least having a lover, for living alone above a store on the main street of a nowhere town, for having no reason to be alive.

I sit at my window and look down along the line of gas lamps that light this town and I do not understand how this growing older has happened. My life has crept up on me somehow, taken me unawares, as if I have been pushing along all this while, young and bright and full of promise and then one morning I awake to find that my life has settled in around me like fat, like cement, that I do not like the person I've become and that it is too late to change that now. I do not want all my energy going into my students and their lives; I do not want to be an old-maid schoolteacher. And I do not know just when this image of myself as a fresh and independent woman solidified into that of a spinster, someone to pity, someone to ask after around the holidays because she has nowhere to go — I am tired of being lonely, being empty; I am tired of dying inside, feeling like my body and my spirit are decaying while I continue to stand upright, continue to function. I watch the lights of the street below and I think of the vet, at home with her family, her husband and her daughter; of Liz, at home with hers; I think of all those people on the street beneath my window going home to their houses, their spouses, their lives, and I realize that I have become lonely, denying all along that it was happening.

I go to bed with Maurice without turning on the lights. I light the candles, try to read my book, but I can't concentrate. Lying back against my pillows, with Maurice warm against my side, I think of Liz, with her olive skin and her deep hazel eyes and her beautiful directness. I slip my hand between my legs and bring myself to a climax so intense that tears fill my eyes, and I am thinking of Liz, for lack of anyone else to think about, when through the haze comes the ringing of the phone, and then my mother's voice, coming soft through the wire, punctuated with static, telling me my father is dead.

fifteen

December 1988   When I pull into the driveway my heart contracts. My parents' house looks the same as it always has; the lighted windows glow in the darkness. It feels like home, though I don't know what home I could be thinking of. It feels familiar, the rows of pine trees that hide it from the road, the curtains that hang in the windows, the trees that surround the house. I pull up in front and turn off the engine. For a moment I think I cannot bear to get out of the car, then I want to fling open the door and run up the front steps and throw myself into my mother's arms. But that is only a dream. This is not my home. This is only the house where I grew up. I am here for only one reason, to close the book on it.

My mother greets me at the door. She looks the same as she did the last time I saw her, except that the hair brushed back from her face is grayer now, and a few more broken blood vessels crisscross her cheeks. Her eyes are level, her hand steady on the doorknob. "It's good to see you," she says. "Come in."

I follow her into the house, holding my suitcase against me like a shield. The house looks just the same inside, too; it still fills me with the same dark emptiness. It is as full of mourning as it always was. No one else is here: only my mother and I, alone together.

"Are you hungry?" my mother says, and I shake my head. It is late; I want only to sleep. I want only to close my eyes and shut my mind off. I want only to be alone.

She takes me upstairs to my old room, overlooking the driveway. "Do you need anything?" she asks me.

"No, thanks," I say, and set my suitcase on the bed.

She pauses for a moment in the doorway. "It's been a long time," she says.

I shrug, flip open the locks on my suitcase.

"Honey," my mother says, but I don't let her finish.

"I'm tired," I say. "Can we talk in the morning?"

Her face sags, like it's fallen in on itself. I harden myself against the sight, against the smell of her powder, the roses of her in the air. "Of course," she says. "Good night." She closes the door behind her, leaving me to my memories, leaving me alone with my ghosts.

As I close my eyes I think how much better I sleep in the rooms of strangers. It is a long time before I fall asleep, and when I do I dream of Colin walking through the woods, red-cheeked and full of laughter, and I think that I hear Zach up ahead, but when I look back Colin is gone and I am all alone and in the trees around me I hear my father's laughter, as cold and mocking as the darkness that fills the woods and hides the path to home, and when I wake my heart is beating and the silence all around me is as cold and final as my death.

I am up bright and early the next morning; I don't even eat breakfast, just put on my clothes and drive to the airport to pick up Zach. Colin will be coming in a few hours; his wife and kids will meet us at the funeral home. Our father's funeral is at noon; we all seem to have planned our arrivals so that we spend as little time here as possible. I wonder what it means that I was the first to get here.

The airport is filled with families reunited for the holidays, hugging beneath the tinsel and fake pine garlands. In a smiling crowd of package-carrying people, I know Zach immediately.

It is like meeting the protagonist of a novel that I've read over and over again. He gets off the plane wearing a blue down jacket and carrying an overnight bag. He has thick black hair and a beard. His face is unforgiving, and when he looks at me I find that I suddenly have nothing to say.

Zach hands me his bag and looks at me through big dark eyes that can't see me while he wipes his glasses with a bandanna he's pulled from the back pocket of his jeans. In the light of the airport his eyes look blue. I'd thought they were brown, but they're not. His beard is thick and full and covers most of his face.

We survey each other solemnly: he is taller than I am, taller than my father was. His shoulders are broad beneath his jacket. He shifts them now and clears his throat. "So," he says. "How are you?" He has an accent; he sounds like he just came in from Scotland. He seems entirely foreign to me, and it occurs to me that we share nothing but blood — we have no common memories.

"Fine," I say. "How are you?" My voice sounds absurdly formal, even to me.

Zach looks around and sighs. "I had a hell of a time getting across the border," he says. "I didn't think at first they were going to let me in." He pulls out his handkerchief again, blows his nose. He looks around us at the smiling, laughing Christmas crowd, stuffs the handkerchief back into his pocket. "I hope to god they let me back out," he says.

We walk through the airport side by side. He wears hiking boots that hit the pavement like mortar fire. He looks like he's from another time, a time when Men were Men; he looks like he's just come down from the hills. He's clearly unused to being around so many people.

He keeps his bag with him in the front seat of the car. Our breath clouds the windows while the car warms up. Zach rubs his clean and looks out while I shift into gear, back the car up through the slush. A family walks past, the parents' arms around each other, the kids carrying packages. Behind us the runway lights fade slowly, lost in the morning sun.

I have no idea what to say to him. I've dreamt about this moment for such a long time, fantasized about it, but now I can think of nothing to say to the real Zach, who looks alarmingly like all the pictures I have formed of him throughout the years. I feel I know more about him than he could ever tell me. I have expected him to know all the answers, to be able to tell me why my life has gone the way it has, but now that I have him here before me, I can't think of anything to ask. We don't talk; I am conscious only of the cold of the steering wheel beneath my hand and him sitting there looking out of the window as we drive the road home, to the place where we grew up.

The snow is piled up on both sides of the road. They plow it every morning, but still there is barely one lane clear as I drive through the falling snow with Zach in the car beside me. I wait for him to speak and he says nothing, only stares through the window with his hand on his chin. I wait for him to ask about our mother, or about me, but he is silent. I start to speak but realize that I do not even know what he does up there, and so I too stay silent, watch the snow resume its fall against the windshield.

I pull into the driveway with Zach and the pine trees float beside us like parting seas. I turn off the engine and neither of us moves for a moment. I keep one hand on the wheel and one on the key in the ignition, as if afraid I'll have to turn it on again in a second. Beside me, Zach is leaning forward, peering through the windshield. We sit in the car in front of the house and around us there is snow on the ground and I can feel Zach beside me, looking. His voice is quiet, like he isn't even talking to me.

"I didn't remember it being so small," he says. I look at him, but he is taking his bag from the floor and opening the door.

In the house Zach doesn't even get his jacket off before my mother throws her arms around him and buries her head in his chest. I watch them for a moment. I wonder if this has been hard for her, to be separated for so long from her own child. I wonder why she never went against my father, why she had to wait until he died. I watch her hug Zach, pressing against him as if he will save her. I wonder why Zach is the one who merits such a greeting. I wonder if it's because she doesn't know him, has no idea who he is.

Zach just stands there with his arms around her and his bag on the floor beside him, looking at the walls. "I thought it was bigger," he says. He walks from room to room with my mother holding his hand and stares at the walls: "I just ... for some reason I thought it was bigger than this," he says, again.

We are at the doorway of the living room when we hear Colin clearing his throat inside. Zach lets go of my mother's hand and looks at the doorway as if he's afraid that Colin will materialize there.

My mother shakes her head. "He *ran* here," she says, as if it were the most ridiculous thing in the world. Her lips are pursed. I wonder why she cares. I wonder if she's afraid people in town will start to talk. Zach looks at me, and then he takes a breath and walks into the living room.

Colin is stretching out before the fireplace, his back to the door, in a runner's ending stretch, his hands pressing the board of his body away from the wall. When I see him, something in my throat catches, as if at any moment I might cry. His legs are all muscle, his whole body is muscle, but there is no shape to him, as if his body has grown around him like the bark of a tree around a nail. Standing there with Zach, I feel like Colin's so far away I'll never reach him.

Zach, still in his coat, fills the doorway with his shoulders; Colin, by the fireplace, is one long string of sinew flickering in the late-morning light that streams in through the windows. There is so little flesh on him, I think if I touched him my hands would go right through. He hasn't seen us yet; his back is to us as he thrusts his body against the mantelpiece and the muscles stand out around the bones of his spine. His body is beautiful in this moment; seeing him now, I realize that he should have been an athlete. He should never have gone to work in a bank, wearing suits that never fit him, that emphasized the roundness of his back, the sloping shoulders. He should have been an athlete; he should have been a runner all along. He never should have had to have another job. I look at Zach and his eyes are dark behind his glasses as he turns to go back into the kitchen. He is gone before Colin even knows he is there.

I stand and look at Colin until he straightens and looks over at me. He looks the same as always, with perhaps the smallest bit of gray in his hair. He doesn't look like a man with two sons, one a musician, the other a computer wiz. He looks like Colin, taking me for a walk in the woods at sunset, but when I move to him and put my arms around him his muscle does not give.

*

My father doesn't seem to have changed at all, laid out in his coffin at the funeral home. He could have been dead the whole time, for all the difference it makes in his appearance. I stand beside the coffin with my mother, Zach, and Colin, and my father lies before us flat on his back, his arms folded on his chest, a scowl on his face.

"I'm sorry about that," the funeral director says, apologetically, edging up to us. "We just couldn't get his face to *do* anything else."

None of us speaks; we don't even look at one another. I am afraid that I will start to laugh. Then I am afraid that I will start to cry, that if I have to stand here one more moment, looking down at his unrelenting, scornful face, I will burst into tears, without even knowing what I am mourning. Surely he wouldn't have wanted to be displayed this way, laid out to be looked at. He spent so much of his life trying not to be seen. I suspect he is relieved to be going underground.

I glance surreptitiously at the rest of my family; they are all just standing there, looking down at him. Zach clears his throat, looks at his watch. "So," he says. "Are we going to get this show on the road?"

We all look at him for a moment. For a second he reminds me of my father, but I put it from me.

The funeral is short, to the point. The few mourners file into the room and find seats. Some of them I recognize. I spot Mrs. Dewberry right away. She looks exactly the same as she did that day in church, interrogating me over the grape juice left over from communion. Mr. Burgess from the grocery store sits at the back. Others look vaguely familiar. I wonder what they're all doing here. I can't imagine that my father would have considered them *friends*. For a moment I resent their presence. What right have they to mourn?

Colin's wife and children slip in just before the service starts; we all sit staring straight ahead throughout the eulogy. This preacher is different from the one from my childhood; he is younger, flashier, more styled, but even his slick delivery cannot distract me from the smell of my father in his coffin, and I think suddenly of Renee's funeral. I think of her lying sedately in the pink satin lining of her coffin, her wrists adeptly hidden beneath a corsage of flowers. Her hair was curled all around her head, spread about her shoulders. There was a look of peace on her face, a look of acceptance that I used to catch on her face often in life. These undertakers are not so bad at what they do; they know how to preserve the persona as well as the body. Or maybe we're just tougher than we think, our faces less elastic than we like to think. Underneath it all, there was still this smell, coming through the embalming fluid. I smell it now, though I suppose it could be my imagination. Smelling it now, coming from my father's coffin, drives home to me again that people don't just die; they rot, first.

🔊

We stand in a single ring around the open grave, watching the cemetery workers lower my father's coffin into it. The early-afternoon sun is almost obscenely bright; it sparkles on the snow that covers the other graves. I stand between Zach and Colin, with Colin's wife and sons on his other side and my mother next to Zach. None of us speaks to one another; I can't imagine what there is to say. Couldn't have hoped for better weather? I stand with my hands folded in front of me. My father is lying down there, entombed in a box for eternity. I can feel something in me begin to shake. I wonder if he's happy now. I wonder if he's finally gotten what he always seemed to want — to be free of us, to be free of this world that seemed to give him so much pain. I wonder where he is. I wonder where Renee is. I stand there in the cemetery, surrounded by the remainder of my family, and I wonder how soon we will have to go through this again.

We wait for the first spadeful of dirt to strike the coffin lid, and then we walk back to our cars, drive out of the cemetery. We leave the graves behind us, get on with our living.

🔊

When we reach the house, Zach and I head for the cupboard above the icebox at the same time. He pours a whiskey, adds some water and ice, and hands it to me. Colin does not drink; he fusses around my mother, who goes to her chair at the dining room table and sits in it, heavily. Zach leans against the kitchen sink, one arm braced behind him, the other holding his glass. Colin's wife, Ruth, moves through the room like an automaton, pouring herself a glass of water without saying a word, not even that she's sorry; she just fills her glass and leaves. Zach and I, in turn, say nothing to her; we only stand there, side by side against the sink, drink our whiskey, and refill our glasses. I wish that Colin would drink with us, but he doesn't even look at us, just heads out of the kitchen, looking for Ruth. I watch him go and feel angry. Why doesn't he look for me?

The living room fills slowly with distant relatives and friends, most of whom I have never seen, and none of whom, I'm sure, would ever have come to see my father when he was still alive, any more than the rest of us would have.

Zach builds a fire in the fireplace. I watch him leaning into the fire, rearranging the wood with my father's poker. From this angle, he could almost be my father; there is that same slant to his face, the same darkness in it. But maybe it's the whiskey, going to my head. He glances up at me. "So," he says, "what is it that you do?"

Zach has a roofing business and lives alone in a cabin in northwestern Alberta. He has no running water or electricity, but he keeps a rain barrel beneath the gutter spout, and limes his outhouse regularly. The neighbors give him ice from their freezers. He reads by kerosene lantern, listens to the news on the radio in his truck as he is making his runs around the territory. He has lived like this for years. "I sent you some letters," he says, not looking at me. He straightens up and walks to the window, looks out across the field. "Didn't you ever get them?" he asks.

I think of my father waving his hand in dismissal; I think of him now sunk six feet into the ground, and I know, for sure, that he is smiling. Outside, a wind is picking up; it swirls the snow in the yard, shakes the branches of the pine trees. "No," I say. "I never did."

Zach continues staring out the window, then looks around for his drink. "Maybe it's just as well," he says. "I didn't really know who I was writing to anyway."

I don't reply, just stand and stare out at the field, flat as ice. It looks like a moat, between us and the woods. I wonder what it would take to drop the drawbridge, let us back into our past. He didn't know who he was writing to. I think that if my father weren't already dead, I'd kill him.

We are still standing there when Colin walks up, his shoulders awkward in his suit, his head bent, his hair as short as if he'd just gotten out of the Corps yesterday, instead of some sixteen, seventeen years ago. He walks up to us with that smile on his face that I remember so well, and for a moment I do not want to acknowledge him in front of Zachary, for a second I am almost embarrassed to have him for my brother. I forget he belongs to Zach as well.

He and Zachary look at each other, check each other out; neither one says anything. Colin looks at me. "Gosh," he says. "Isn't it great that there's so many people here?" Zach and I just look at him. "Maura," Colin says, "how have you been?"

I look at him, at him and Zach, standing before me. There could be a cliff between us; they seem so far away. Deep inside, I can feel something shift, as if that anger I have stored within me is coming back to life, slowly, cell by cell. I look at Colin, at his blank, pale face, his blinking eyes. What does he mean? He knows about Magdelene, he knows about Renee. I wrote him letter after letter. Doesn't he remember? What does he mean, how have I been? I've lost everything, twice. What am I supposed to say? Things are moving inside me, in that shifting that precedes an avalanche. I try to breathe deeply, shut it down, keep everything in place. "Okay," I say. My teeth feel glued together. "What about you?"

"Oh, great," he says, "just great," and in the pause that follows I can see that nothing has changed. My Colin is still missing; this Colin has no clue. I look at him and my heart aches and I think that the hurt will never stop. He really doesn't know, has no idea who I am. I think I cannot bear it. Zach excuses himself, goes into the kitchen to get another drink. Colin and I drift out to the back porch, stand by the window overlooking the field. "You used to write the greatest letters," Colin says. "Do you remember them? You used to write the longest letters of anyone I know."

I look at him and I want to cry; I want to cry for the person who no longer writes letters, who no longer knows how to keep contact with the people she ought to love; I want to cry for this man who never knew how to write her back. He stands there before me, bland-faced, seeming empty of emotion. I want him back. I want to talk to him. "How are you, Colin?" I ask again, forgetting that I just asked him. Please, I think, please tell me how you really are. Oh, please be real with me. I think I can forgive him anything, if he'll only give me the truth.

"Ruth wants a divorce," Colin tells me. "She doesn't want the kids. She's been to a psychiatrist; he says she's depressed." We are standing beside my father's chair, the chair he used to sit in to watch the sun set, night after night, alone with his beer. "I've been doing the same job for the last seventeen years," Colin tells me.

He stops then, and I'm not sure what to say. "How do you feel about that?" I ask him, lamely.

Colin looks at me and laughs, and for a second I see him at seventeen, a red-cheeked boy with dark blond hair. "How do you think I feel?" he says. "I'm bored out of my mind."

Standing there next to him, I wonder suddenly what it is to have that kind of boredom, instead of my own. Colin stares out across the field. "We used to go for walks," he says. "Do you remember?"

Do I remember. I look out with him at the field of our childhood. The drawbridge is up; there is no access. I will never get back there. I will never get back to my life. Beside me, Colin sighs and shifts his weight. Do I remember. I look at that field, naked in its winter bareness, and I think that I remember everything all the time, and I think that all I remember is losing him, and losing Zach, and losing that little girl who drowned her people in the creek, dusted off her hands, and went back home, for dinner.

Zach brings me another drink, and the three of us stand together for a moment, before the window. Do we resemble one another? I wonder. Do we share any similarities? Standing there between them I wonder suddenly who I am. What do I want from life?

I look back into the living room at Colin's kids, who stand forlornly by the fireplace. They are beautiful children. One has Colin's yellow hair. The other is dark. Both have skin that is smooth and free of blemishes. "Will's flunking out of school," Colin says. "He won't write his essays; he turns the papers in blank, with only his name at the top of the page. Reuben plays the violin, but that's all he wants to do." Colin sighs, puts his hands in his pockets. "He practices all the time, instead of doing his homework."

I look again at the kids by the fireplace. Their open faces are somber, vulnerable; they look lost. Will stands before the fire, a dark and silent presence, his eyes downcast. Reuben stands behind him, his musician's fingers resting lightly on the mantelpiece as he stares into the flames. Looking at them before the fire, I think of myself at that age, playing my games, making up my stories. What kind of kids are they, what do they like to do? They stand there not a room's length from me, already adolescents, and I realize that I have no idea who they are, these nephews of mine.

❧

Some woman comes over to us, grips first my hands, then Zach's, then Colin's. Her fingers ooze in ours. "So sorry," she says, whispering, "so very sorry about your father." I have no idea who she is. Mrs. Dewberry comes up next, aging, heavyset. She takes my hand in both of hers, holds it, beaming.

"I bet you don't remember me," she says, smiling coyly.

"Sure I do," I say. "How could I forget?" The irony is clearly lost on her. She beams at me, squeezes my hand in hers.

"You've certainly grown up," she says. "We hear good things about you."

She hears good things about me. I can feel myself start to tremble; I can feel a pressure building in my chest. How dare she hear things about me, how dare she think of me at all. I think of Mrs. Dewberry sitting in church, grape juice trickling from the corners of her mouth like blood. I feel the blood leave my head. That shaking that began as I stood over my father's grave is stirring inside my chest. I look at Mrs. Dewberry, but she has dropped my hand and turned to Colin, patting him sloppily on the shoulder.

"Such lovely children," she says, "so accomplished."

Then she turns to Zach. She is like a panther, zeroing in on her prey. Her eyes narrow; I almost think I see her ears go flat. "And Zach," she says. "I've heard so much about you." She takes his hand and strokes it, looks up into his face with innocent, panther eyes. She is stalking him. "We missed it so much," she says, "getting to know you." She smiles up at him. "Where was it that you went to?" she asks. "All those years ago?"

I can feel the wind getting stronger out in the field; the trees are lifting with it, their trunks bending to its rhythm. I can feel it pick up as it moves across the field, becoming nearly a tornado as it reaches the house. I can sense the clouds thickening in the sky, I can see the funnel drop from them, I can see it coming across the field, heading straight for us. There is no escaping it. Behind us a shutter bangs; Mrs. Dewberry jumps.

"Hey," I say to Mrs. Dewberry, suddenly, loudly. Heads lift around the room. "Hey," I say, and the voices around us hush as if choked. Silence fills the room. Mrs. Dewberry peers up at me, both of her hands still encircling Zach's, as if she had his neck between them. Her face is a blank white slate. How dare she touch us? How dare she presume to lay her hands on us. The shaking in me has taken on shape, taken on a presence. It has become a hawk, lifting its wings in me. It soars within me, its head in mine; it soars and spots its prey and drops like a bolt of lightning, talons open. "Fuck you," I say to Mrs. Dewberry. "Fuck you to hell," and as I say it the wind overtakes the room, lifting papers and books and the hems of women's skirts. "Get out of our house," I say to her. I step toward her and she backs away. I lift my wings and set my talons in her chest; with my beak I tear out her throat. Zach looks at me, startled, but in Colin's eyes I catch a gleam of my father, a gleam of his approval, and as Mrs. Dewberry and the others turn and run, I swallow her flesh and take my flight again, leave them behind, rent and emptied of their power.

🐦

Will shows me the Nintendo he brought with him, shows me how to play one of the games. We kill bugs on the screen for a while. Reuben shows me his violin, plays Mozart for me, in Colin's old bedroom, away from the anxious hush down-stairs. Their heads bow over their projects, dark and light together, here where their father used to sleep. I watch them showing me their things and it suddenly occurs to me how much I have missed. All this time my family has been living their lives, while I shut mine down by my own hand, consigning myself to my own limbo, worse than any the nuns could have dreamed of.

🐦

"Listen," Zach says, finding me upstairs in the room that used to be mine, standing beside the bed with its worn pink quilt. "I know you've got a job and all," he says. "I know I don't have much to offer, but I'd like it if you'd come and live with me for a while — I have the lumber for another cabin; we could build it on another part of my land, so you could have your privacy."

I look at him; I study his face with its hard lines, its fierce blue eyes. I look at his hard, compact body, his roofer's hands. I think of him up there in the solace of his land and in that moment I want nothing more than to forget my job and my apartment, and take my things and go with him, north to where his home is now. I look out at the driveway, at the basketball net dangling limply from its hoop. I look at Zach and for a moment it is my father standing there, his eyes on mine. I shake my head and it is Zach again, his eyes as opaque as standing water, and it seems suddenly that there is no decision to be made.

"Yes," I say. "I'll come with you."

❧

Downstairs my mother is seeing off the last of the neighbors and distant relatives. She makes a pot of tea, sits at the table to drink it, opens up one of the casseroles that the women has brought, and makes a face. I sit down beside her.

She doesn't look at me. "All these casseroles are pork and sausage," she says. "Don't these people have cholesterol to worry about? Look at this," she says, peeling back the foil, "all this cheese. It's awful, isn't it?" She sits and looks at the casserole for a moment, and then her shoulders start to shake and I think at first that she is laughing, but she drops her head into her hands and I see that she is crying, there at the head of her table. "You're all here," she says, "you're all finally here, but no one made their peace with him — you all just came to bury him." She looks up at me. "Why couldn't you come back a little sooner?" she asks me. "He wanted to see you. He talked about you all the time. He loved you."

I can feel something in me closing, as if my throat were collapsing in on itself. "Oh, bullshit," I say. I can hardly get the words out. I feel like I cannot breathe. "He didn't give a shit about me." I suddenly think that I will cry.

My mother sets her cup down. Her face is drawn, the skin lined with wrinkles that slice her face at every angle. "Do you know," she says, as if she hasn't heard me, "that after Dan left, when the boys were gone, I used to sit here and sometimes I could swear I heard that basketball bouncing, just the way it did when Dan was here playing." She lifts her cup again, but the tea is gone and she sets the cup back down. "I told your father that once, not too long ago." She looks past me, out the window, at the birds that cluster around the feeder.

"He said he'd heard it, too," she says. "All that time he'd heard it, too."

The room is silent, drowned in the light of dusk. The wind is dying down; the trees are nearly quiet now, their bare branches stripped of the snow that clung to them earlier. I think of the basketball net, limp on its hoop. All those nights in my room, drawing pictures, writing stories, reading books, I never heard it. All those silent days and nights, when I was mourning Magdelene, when I was mourning Colin, when I was mourning Zach, they were mourning Dan, somebody else's kid.

"All those paper people you used to make," my mother says, "all those family stories you used to write — I always wondered why you didn't give your own family the same attention."

The anger surges up in me so suddenly that I think I will choke on it. "What are you talking about?" My head is buzzing; I feel like I'm on fire. "What about *your* family? What about Zach and Colin?" I think I cannot breathe; my anger is rising so high and fast that I think I will drown in it. "What about *me?*" I ask her. "You ruined my life — you took Magdelene away from me, Miss Greenway—"

My mother pushes back her chair. "Stop it," she says. Her face is flushed, as if with wine. "Just stop it." She picks her empty cup up; it shakes in her hand. "I've had enough," she says, and her voice is rising, scaling upward, till I think her words will hit the ceiling, rain down on us like fallout. "I can't do this with you right now." She is nearly shrieking now; I think the cup will break in her hands. She turns away from me, walks out into the kitchen, stands with her back to me. "You'll never understand," she says, biting off her words and spitting them out, "what it was like for me."

I follow her; I think that I will seize her shoulders, turn her around, force her to face me. "What it was like for *you,*" I say. "Why don't you ask me about my life?" I no longer feel like I'm choking. My throat is wide open, like a field, like the sky. "I've buried a lover; I found her body. I loved her."

"Well, how was I supposed to know?" my mother asks me. "You never told me about it. You just left."

"I didn't leave," I say. "You threw me out." My anger is huge inside of me. It lifts me, till I fill the doorway, crowd it with my shoulders. "I want to tell you about it," I say. "I want you to hear about it now. I wasn't making families — I only made those people to burn them. That was all I ever did with them. I never played with them," I say.

"Yes," she says, putting her teacup in the sink, so hard that I think it will shatter. She turns to face me. Her hair clings to her forehead; her face is twisted, ugly with her grief. "I know," she says. "I know the way you played."

❧

Colin sees Ruth off in her car after the wake; upstairs, the boys stay ensconced in his old room, playing their pieces and Nintendo games. Colin stands in the doorway, watching his wife drive off. Outside, the wind is still; the trees stand motionless, like soldiers at attention. The sun is setting; its colors stain the sky. My father's sun, setting without him. I can hear Zach on the stairs, bringing down his bag. My mother doesn't look at me, walks back out into the dining room, sinks into her chair.

"I can't believe he's leaving already," she says. "I can't believe he'd come all that way and not stay a few days."

"What should he hang around here for?" I ask her. "What is there for him here? What is there here for any of us?" I look at her, sitting in her chair. "I'm going with him," I tell her. "I'm going back with him." But my mother only sits in her place at her end of the table across from an empty chair. She doesn't say a word to me. All around us everything is quiet. The house resounds with my father's absence.

Zachary comes into the room, his overnight bag in his hand. "Ready to go?" he says to me.

My mother doesn't move from her chair, but Colin and his sons are already on the front porch, ready to see him off. I look at my mother, where she sits with her head down and her hands folded, surrounded by foil-covered casseroles. The light of the setting sun glints through the window behind her head and catches the gray in her hair and for a moment I want to go to her, I want to touch her hair, touch the veins that line her cheeks. I want to kneel beside her and put my head in her lap and start all over, do it all again, do everything differently, but there's a hardness in my stomach like a bolt slammed shut. I get up and walk to the front door, where my bags stand waiting. For a moment I think of Maurice, stretching fatly in his kennel at the married vet's. The boys stand awkwardly on the porch, in pants that are too short for them. I look at them and I want to go out and put my arms around them, take them out and buy them clothes that fit, cook them dinner. I want to take them out and show them my woods, show them all my secret hiding places, but I'm no longer sure that I could find them. The drawbridge is up; there is no return. We are all sealed here in this moment of transition, waiting to move into our future.

I walk out to my car and open the passenger side for Zach. He throws his bag in the backseat and gets in the front, sits there, firm and strong and competent, full of body. On the front porch, Colin stands hunched with his sons at his side, the smile gone from his face. He looks like a little boy; he looks younger than his sons. I look at Colin and I want to go to him and take his hand and tell him all about my life. I look at Zach and I look at Colin and I do not want to have to choose between them. I want them both. I want it all. I think I cannot bear this.

I look at Colin and I look at his sons and when I look up at my mother's window I see her looking down at me, her face almost invisible behind the glass. She could be a picture, standing there. The world is still. For the first time, I am the one that is leaving. Why do I feel so empty?

I get into the car. Behind me the house looms like a mausoleum. I glance back up at Colin on the porch. I start the engine, and from the corner of my eye I see a hand waving me away, a shoulder shutting me out. The wind ripples the grass. I can hear the softness of the basement door as it closes, finally, endlessly. "Let's go," I say.

🐦

The drive to the airport takes forever. We are going to redeem his ticket and then take off, drive my car to his cabin in Alberta. Drive to my new life. I try not to think of Maurice, or of my students. Zach cracks the window open, lights a cigarette. "I can't believe those people," he says. "Colin," he says, and snorts a little, the way my father used to. "He must belong to some other family." He shakes his head in disgust. The smoke from his cigarette fills the car, floods it with his scorn.

I keep my hands on the wheel, keep driving, keep breathing. Within my chest, my hawk is fluttering its wings, pecking at my insides, seeking exit.

"And Mother," Zach says. "Christ. She's got no backbone at all," he says. He could be my father, the way he sounds. I don't even hear the accent anymore. I hear only my father's voice, my father's anger. Zachary didn't escape this place any more than I did. He is not the character that I created for him, finding liberation in the fierce north wind. He is only Zach, roofing houses in the cold, making do in the place where he has found himself. And suddenly I know what I have to do.

Magdelene is gone. Renee is dead. I will never see them again. For a moment I feel the anguish rise in me, and I want to trample it, stamp it down inside me, put it out like a fire. But I take my panic and I put it from me. I take a deep breath and I steady myself and I let my anguish rise, let it roll through me like a wave, disappearing out to sea. They are gone, but I am here. I am alive. I am still present in my life. I can live my life for myself.

I pull into the airport, idle the car beside the ticket door. "I'm not going with you," I say. "I'm staying where I am."

Zach looks at me. "You sure?" he says, one hand on the door latch.

I nod. "I'm sure," I say. "I'd like to visit you," I tell him, but he is already out of the car, his overnight bag on the sidewalk beside him.

He leans back in before shutting the door. "Okay," he says. "Whatever you want."

"This is what I want," I say, and as I say it I think that I have never felt so sure of anything before. I get out of the car, walk around to Zachary, and hold him tight in my arms. His body is stiff in my embrace, and again I think how much he is like my father, how much we are all, despite ourselves, like our father.

"Good-bye, then," he says, and picks up his bag.

"Good-bye," I say, and watch him stride through the door without looking back. For a moment something surges up in me again, that wave of emptiness, that ragged, tearing pain around my heart that reminds me that recovery will be slow. I want him to fight for me. I do not want him to give me up so easily. I watch his back, straight and stiff, as he walks away from me, loses himself within the crowd of people heading for their planes. He never looks back. I stand there and I take a deep breath, feel cold December air flood my lungs. It braces me. I close my eyes and take it into me like communion, breathe of its body and its blood, take my strength from it. I get back into my car, put it into gear, and pull away from the curb. As I leave the airport, I tap the horn, lightly, hear its echo in the air as I leave the airport behind, start the long drive back to Pennsylvania. I will go back to the place that has become my home, to my tiny mountain town. I will go back to my job at my little college in the hills. I will go back to teaching my students. I will tell them to pick colors, take walks, write down what they're thinking. And then I'll call on them to read. I will pick up Maurice, spring him from the kennel. I will say hello to Earl, open the door, and let the air back into my apartment. But the first thing I will do when I get back is look for Liz, who will no longer be my student.

As I pull out onto the highway, the hawk within me lifts its wings and soars away, back into its sky, and I think as it goes that I see Magdelene's slow wink, Renee's wistful smile, in the sky that opens up to take it in, and as I drive I feel within me the rhythm of my beating heart, cycling blood back through my veins, giving me my life, the one that I've been living all this time.

*Alyson Publications publishes a wide variety
of books with gay and lesbian themes. For a free catalog
or to be placed on our mailing list, please write to:*

Alyson Publications
40 Plympton Street
Boston, MA 02118

*Indicate whether you are interested in books for
gay men, lesbians, or both.*